T0063004

TREASURE ON
BEAVER ISLAND

LLOYD HARNISHFEGER

Order this book online at www.trafford.com
or email orders@trafford.com

Most Trafford titles are also available at major online book retailers.

© Copyright 2013 Lloyd Harnishfeger.
All rights reserved. No part of this publication may be reproduced, stored in a retrieval
system, or transmitted, in any form or by any means, electronic, mechanical, photocopying,
recording, or otherwise, without the written prior permission of the author.

Printed in the United States of America.

ISBN: 978-1-4907-1496-7 (sc)
ISBN: 978-1-4907-1497-4 (e)

Trafford rev. 09/20/2013

www.trafford.com

North America & international
toll-free: 1 888 232 4444 (USA & Canada)
fax: 812 355 4082

For Leah

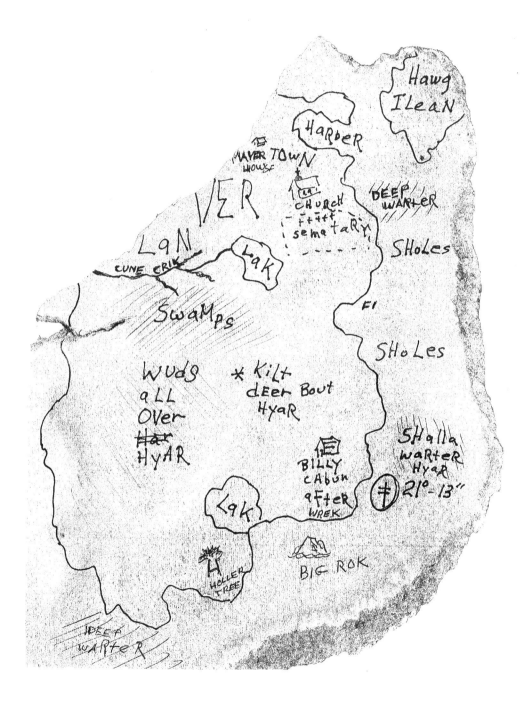

CONTENTS

CHAPTER ONE

Secret in the Gun

Ed was sitting hunched over on the old milk can, staring at the ancient muzzle loader. Almost as tall as the sixteen-year-old himself, it was hanging on two nails behind the stove, its curly maple stock glistening in the light from a small window. The boy had never allowed even a speck of dust to remain on the gun for long. He handled it often, but always carefully replaced it on the nails.

"That old gun has to be the answer!" he told himself aloud, staring at it almost angrily. "Why didn't you just tell the whole story? Your diary is plenty clear about everything else you did back in those days! Logging, running freight in that side-wheeler you were on, all that stuff is written down, so why couldn't you have told us where the treasure is? And while you were at it, how about *what* it is?"

He stood, dusted his pants and reached for the old rifle. It was a heavy weapon, probably fifty caliber or more. The ramrod was missing and there was no flint in the lock. Ed didn't like to look at the lock much. He had traded off the original flint two years ago. Just another of the many things he wished he hadn't done.

The boy picked up the three-eighths inch dowel rod he'd bought at the general store. A final inspection proved the wood to be smooth, and the linseed oil on it looked like it had finally dried. "I hope this thing is long enough," he mumbled. "It better be, it cost me seven cents!" Money was short there on the farm in 1946. He had spent the rest of his change on a package of "walnettos" to eat on the way home from the Blue Lick general store.

He sighted along the four foot wooden shaft and found it straight enough. A piece of clean cloth, soaked with "Haleys # 10" bore cleaner, slipped into a slot he'd made in the end of the rod. It made a fair patch. He was ready! So far as he knew the barrel had never been cleaned and he was finally going to do it. If it worked, his plan was to use the same dowel as a makeshift ramrod. "If everything works out," he told himself, "I intend to learn to shoot this old weapon!" This was never to happen.

The wooden shaft with its dripping linen patch fitted snugly enough to suit the boy. With the gun stock resting on the floor, gently but firmly he pressed the rod down, turning it a little with every inch. Drawing it back out after only six inches, he was appalled at the amount of rust and dirt on the cloth. The barrel was in much worse shape than he had hoped.

Ed was patient, knowing that the task would take a lot of time. He pressed the dowel down the barrel a little farther, turning it carefully before extracting it. After changing the cloth several times and adding more bore cleaner he could tell he was now only about ten inches from the length of the barrel.

Then *it happened!*

The homemade cleaning rod struck something solid lodged above the breech. He pushed the rod down several more times but the result was the same. "What the heck is in there?" he mused. There was only one logical answer. A lead rifle ball had been in place for well over a century. Old Eli had rammed the round lead missile down the barrel one last time before he hung the gun up for good.

Ed was puzzled by one thing. Why was the musket ball, if that's what it was, blocking the barrel a good ten inches from the breech? Anyone could tell that the lead should have been further down, only a few inches from the lock and trigger mechanism. The boy's heart began racing as an idea grew in his mind.

"*That's it!*" he whispered. "I knew the old guy's diary hinted that the gun had something to do with the treasure! I've got to read it again! Wish I'd listened better when Mom was reading some of it aloud a year ago."

X   X   X

"No, you *cannot!*" Ed's mother snapped. "The last time I allowed you to read those pages you not only got jelly on one, but you even tore one of them in two. I'm not getting those out again for you to mess with. They've been handed down for three generations, and now they're mine. I've been thinking about donating them to the historical society in Templeton. Maybe they can keep them from falling apart."

"O.K. I did get jam on a page or two, but I never tore any. They're so old and brittle they just sort of fall apart. Mom, I've got to read those diaries again. I've *got to!*"

"What you've got to do now is your chores, boy! Get going." Ed's dad stomped out of the kitchen door, two empty milk pails clanking beside him.

"Aw Mom. . ."

"Maybe sometime if the society doesn't want them," she

offered. "But the chicken coop floor had better be clean enough to eat off by tomorrow."

"Aw Mom. . ."

He pulled on his old work jacket, a hat, and a pair of ragged gloves. It was still cold in March, with the wind making sad moanings as it curled around the kitchen door. His four buckle arctics were in the shed, banished there by his mother. They were cold but he tugged them on over his school shoes. They would warm up soon enough as he worked.

Curly shook her head angrily as the boy dumped a second scoop of chop into her feed box. The jersey didn't like him, and she made that very clear. When she finally settled into her feed he pulled the stool in place and began milking. It was slow work. Ed's dad had already finished his two cows and had gone to feed the hogs. "How am I going to get those diaries without Mom knowing it?" he thought. "Maybe If I can get her out of the front room somehow I could take them out of their little box in the cabinet, put the empty box back, slip them under my shirt, and sneak them up to my bedroom. By golly, that might work!"

As the thick, rich milk struck the side of the bucket his mind was whirling! TREASURE! Old Eli's diary! He had a growing idea that the diary and the long gun somehow held the answer.

BANG! Curly's right hind hoof blasted the bucket from between his knees, and the milk went flying. Scrambling madly he managed to right the pail, but less than a third of the milk was saved. In addition, the bucket showed a deep dent just below the bail. Furiously he punched the cow in the side with his fist. "STUPID COW!" he raged as she flinched from the blow. He knew it was his own fault. Curly had given up all her milk, but with his mind filled with thoughts of a treasure found and great riches realized, he had not stopped trying to get more milk when he should have. Curly was dry! There was nothing to do but face the music. Ed turned the cow out of her stall and headed for the milk house. The pail felt very light in his hand.

Ed's dad was just finishing up when his son slipped inside. He took one look at the boy's face, then an angry glance at the dented and nearly empty milk bucket. He did not ask for an explanation. "Wool gathering again?" he snarled. Without warning his right hand flashed out. He back-handed the boy across the ear, hard enough to set his son reeling. Ed was barely able to keep from spilling what was left in the pail. "Take that to the kitchen!" he said, paying no attention to the red color growing under the boy's ear. "We might as well use it ourselves since there's not enough left to sell." Ed scrambled away, banging the bucket on the door jamb so hard he nearly lost what was left. So upset and angry was he that he forgot about his boots. Two steps onto the kitchen linoleum his mother's shout stopped him.

"Ed! Get back out and leave those boots in the shed like I always tell you! Why are you bringing that milk in here?" He set the pail on the floor and began to back out when she stopped him. "What's the matter with your ear? It's bleeding."

"Curly kicked the bucket," he mumbled, still standing in the half open door. "I lost most of the milk and the pail got dented. Dad whacked me a good one."

"Oh Eddie," she sighed, "Why can't you keep your mind on your work? Ever since you started reading Eli's diaries you've been about half here. Well get on out and change your boots. You're letting the cold in."

Bootless, he came back in and strained the milk into a bowl. He washed the bucket, threw out the round patch of muslin with its collection of what had been in the milk, and washed the strainer. "I've got homework," he said, heading into what they called the "dining room" even though they rarely had a meal there.

"Let me clean that cut," his mother called from the kitchen.

"No Mom, I already washed it off. It's not bleeding anymore." Books on his lap, he settled into the old chair beside the coal stove.

"I'm surprised at you," she said, wiping her hands on her apron. "Tomorrow's Saturday and you're doing homework already. What's going on?"

"Just going to get it done so I can go hunting tomorrow."

Thinking nasty thoughts about the poor lot and unfair treatment of teenagers, he opened the geometry text at random. Scattering a few sheets of yellow tablet paper on his lap, he once again occupied his mind with the *real* problem; how to get his hands on the forbidden, hand-written manuscripts that rested in the cabinet just a few feet away. No new theories presented themselves so he faked studying for another half hour.

He rose, gathered up the untouched papers and closed his textbook. It had been too warm by the stove, but that would not be a problem much longer. His trap line was over a mile long and the temperature was already in the single digits.

"Finished your homework already?"

"Yeah, Mom, I'm done with it for tonight. I'll be back by ten at the latest."

"If you're going to check your traps, first you'd better tell your dad you're sorry about the milk."

"Well I've got a *sore ear!* Isn't that enough? Do I have to apologize too, for Pete's sake?"

"You'd better be careful. If your dad hears you sassing me back like that you'll have a sore something else! He's out in the shop. You can stop in there on your way to the creek."

Ed said nothing but his lips were pressed in a tight line, the way they always did when he was mad.

"Well are you going to do as I said?"

"I'll do it Mom, but it's not fair. That da. . .I mean danged cow is just mean!"

"*Watch your mouth Edward!* You're in enough trouble already.

Get going."

Calvin Nolan was not a big man. Ed was a couple inches taller, but the difference in their heights had nothing to do with which one was boss! The homemade forge was running, its red glow casting wavering highlights on the man's nose and chin.

"Uh . . . Dad, . . I'm . . uh.. sorry about the milk and the bucket...but the bucket's not hurt much. I can still use it. And anyway. ."

"You've got to learn to keep your mind on your work. It's always *something* with you! All summer you were mooning around down along the crick drawing pictures. *Pictures!* What good are they anyway? I expect you to be running this farm someday, so you'd better set your mind on learning how to do it!" He continued bouncing the baby sledge hammer off the red hot plow share he was sharpening.

"I'll do better dad. And I'm sorry."

"Where you off to now? Goin' to check your trap line I suppose. Well at least that pays a little cash money. Next time you sell fur you're to give me eighty-five cents. That'll about cover the cost of the milk you spilled. Now go on."

Ed left the shop without another word. The cold hit hard after the over-heated building. He whistled for Jiggs, but the old dog only stuck his head out of his doghouse for a minute, sniffed the cold air and disappeared. "Smart dog," Ed thought as he headed down the rutted lane toward the stream.

He had twelve muskrat sets under the frozen surface. Each one was marked with a bull thistle he had stuck through the ice and into the mud below. The first marker stood out sharply in the beam of the navy surplus lantern he carried. There was no disturbance in the area around the trap, so there was nothing to do here. His next two sets, about a hundred yards downstream, were close together. One was undisturbed but the second one showed there had been a struggle. It was sprung but empty. Ed drew the hatchet from his belt and broke the ice all the way around the set. The chain was fouled on a tree root and had to be straightened out before he could reset the steel trap and replace it at the edge of the hole.

A little snow was falling as he made his way down his trap line, walking the ice. He was having no success, as five more sets were undisturbed. He wasn't surprised, as the season was nearly over and he had already taken twenty-one of the small fur-bearers from this mile long stretch of the creek. The very last set held a muskrat! One big back foot was deep in the jaws. The creature was dead, drowned when it could not break through the ice.

"Just one," Ed thought sadly. "But if this pelt's as good as the others I've caught this winter it should bring two dollars and twenty cents. Eighty-five cents to Dad will leave me a dollar thirty-five. I'll still have enough for four gallons of gas and a quart of oil. That should keep the old Ford going for a while yet anyway." He began to whistle a tune as he started toward home.

The snow was coming harder as he mushed his way toward the deeper black of the farm buildings. A weak yellow glow from the kitchen window led him to the back of the house. His lantern was getting dimmer as he pushed the shed door open. "Man I hope the batteries last a few more nights," he told himself as he yanked off his boots and coveralls. "Those things cost like the dickens, but trapping is about over, so maybe I'll make it." He dropped the dead rat into an old bushel basket he used for the purpose, but didn't leave the shed right away. He was mulling over the same thing that had been on his mind all the time he was at the creek. He was dreaming up and abandoning a dozen different ploys for sneaking those diaries out of a locked cabinet!

The plan struck him the moment he eased through the kitchen door. "A *lie!*" he thought. "Just a little one ought to do it, but I'll have to wait until Monday." As Ed crept silently up the stairs to his room the excitement was mounting with every step. "Oh *wow!*" he thought. "I'll be reading old Eli's scribbles long before noon on Monday!"

Sleep was impossible as he considered all the angles that would be necessary for his scheme to work. His mom did the washing on Mondays, but before starting on that she always took her eggs to the general store. Ed's dad would have to take her, as she was afraid to drive the truck on snow-covered roads. That meant they would both be gone for at least an hour in the morning. With luck, a safety pin, and a little patience, he should be able to pick the simple lock on the glass cabinet door.

Still wide awake as the downstairs clock struck twelve, he became aware of the wind, which was beginning to howl around the corner of his room. For the first time in all his school years, he hoped that his school *wouldn't* be closed on Monday!

After church on Sundays when his chores were done he was usually free to do whatever he wanted, except drive his new [to him]

1935 Ford. He didn't mind the ruling this time, since he had some serious planning to do.

CHAPTER TWO

The Forbidden Diary

Sunday seemed to last a week. The snow had tapered off during the night but the wind had actually increased. Glumly, Ed peered out at the blowing snow which was building a remarkable drift in the lee of the barn. Chores had been difficult that morning, especially the milking. The cows were nervous because of the wind. The creaking siding boards, shrunken by the cold, made sudden snapping sounds which further agitated the cattle. They were reluctant to "let the milk down", so milking took longer than usual.

Of course Ed had been very careful with his milk pail!

"Stop prowling around the house," his mom said again. "Ever since we got home from church you've hardly sat down at all. Except for when you gobbled all that chicken. What *is* the matter with you?"

"Uh . . . I guess it's the storm. Do you think they'll call off school tomorrow?"

"Nobody will be going anywhere tomorrow!" his dad pronounced, without appearing from behind his newspaper. "Ed, I'll need your help tomorrow. Two jobs that have to be done."

"What jobs?"

"We need to move a lot of coal from the coal shed into the cellar. The way this winter's going the stuff just seems to disappear."

"But Dad, how can we run a wheelbarrow through all this snow?" Ed complained.

"There's a wonderful invention called a snow shovel. We'll make a path first."

"What's the other job?" Ed asked as he left the window and headed for the stairs. "There was no reason for him to get so smart," he thought as he flopped onto his unmade bed. "He always has to make me look stupid. Well I'll show him. There's a treasure to be found and I intend to find it. All I need is to get my hands on those diaries. The answer is in them. I'm sure of it!"

"The other job is mucking out the milking stalls," Cal yelled up the stairs.

His father had been right about the weather. Schools and virtually everything else was shut down, not only on Monday, but Tuesday as well.

On Wednesday most of the major roads had been plowed out. With everything more or less back to normal, Ed knew that it was time to put his plan into action. He was already awake when he heard the alarm clock go off in his parents' bedroom downstairs. He slipped out of bed in the darkness, and felt for his heavy robe. He wrapped himself up in the garment and began a vigorous but silent set of exercises. He kept them up until he heard his mom's voice from below.

"Ed, are you awake? It's chore time. Better hurry or you'll miss the school bus." He didn't answer, but kept the exercises going.

"Eddie, you get up *right now!* I don't have time to come up there and get you."

He still didn't answer. He was doing toe touches as fast as he could until he heard angry steps clomping up the stairs. He threw off the robe and dived under the covers.

"Now Ed, this is about enough . . ." his mother began but stopped when she heard a pitiful moan coming from her son, who lay curled in a fetal position under the quilt.

"I think I'm getting sick," the boy groaned, burying his head in the pillow. "I think I've got a fever. Maybe it's the flu or something."

"Let me see." She turned on the light and placed a cool hand on his forehead. "Maybe a degree or so, but Eddie, you're covered with sweat!"

"I sure feel awful, Mom. Do you think Dad could do my chores this morning?"

"Of course. I'll tell him about you when I gather the eggs. Eddie, as soon as chores are done I have to get to the store. I've got three days' worth of eggs to sell. Dad will need to drive me. We'd be gone for an hour or two. Do you think you'll be o.k. until we get back?"

"I think so," the boy mumbled. "You just go on. I'll be o.k. here, but be sure that Dad takes you. The roads must still be pretty bad."

"Well, if you're sure. Do you want any breakfast?"

"No Mom, I'll just stay right here till you get back. Take your time. I'll be fine, honest." He managed a weak cough or two. "It's a wonder," he told himself grumpily, "that I'm not *really sick* after all the work he dreamed up for me while the schools were closed!" Such thoughts were meant to make him feel better about all the lying. It didn't, but he intended to keep to the plan anyway.

He could monitor every activity that went on as his parents went about their morning work. Milk buckets, clanging against the big milk cans, his mom feeding the chickens then changing into her "better clothes" as she got ready to go to the store. He grinned impishly as the school bus horn beeped twice. He heard the old vehicle start up and move on down the road. "Free!" he thought. "I wish they would finally get going."

"Why am I just lying here?" he asked himself. "I could be up and dressed right now, so I could get to work on that cabinet right away. That would give me a little more time to read the diaries." He was actually half way out of bed when he heard the third stair step creak the way it always did. He dived back under the covers just as his door opened quietly. His mother was standing just inside his room, listening. He did not move. After a moment he heard the door quietly close again. As before, the third step creaked as she made her way back down. Now he could relax.

The old truck started up and continued to idle until his parents were ready to leave. Ed listened until the sound of the truck had faded into the distance. He jumped up, got dressed, and raced downstairs.

The living room was cold, as they kept it closed off during winter months unless company was expected. It was still dark outside, but he only turned on one lamp. With a big safety pin he had straightened out, he began to work on the lock. It didn't budge. He tried bending a tiny hook on the end of the pin, but that didn't work either. Getting a little frustrated, he ran to the bathroom and grabbed one of his mother's bobby pins from the medicine cabinet. Several times he was sure he had it, but this didn't work any better than the safety pin. "*Dang it!*" he said aloud. "If I don't get this thing open pretty soon I won't even have time to read any of old Eli's diaries."

Time was passing and he was no closer to the documents than when he first started. Desperate measures were called for! A quick look down the road assured him that his parents were still gone. Gently but firmly he placed a knee against the cabinet door and began to push. He was delighted when an opening appeared large enough that the locking pin was revealed. Using the point of his homemade tool he eased the little brass tumbler backward. Suddenly the door sprang open, but his knee was still applying pressure. A soft "click" could be heard from the bottom of the glass door. "Oh, NO!" Ed gasped in horror. Forgetting the diaries, he knelt in front of the door and examined the break. A straight crack, perhaps three inches long, was plainly visible at the very bottom of the door.

"Now I've done it!" he groaned. "How could I hide that crack? Mom's sure to see it when she dusts the furniture." He could think of nothing. With his time nearly gone, he had an inspiration. Racing into the dining room he grabbed his school books. A yellow tablet provided plenty of paper. Ripping out a chunk of pages, he ran back to the cabinet and carefully removed the little cedar wood box that held the diaries. Raising the lid, he caught his breath at the sight of the objects he had been thinking about for so long. It had been a long time since his mother had read some of the old man's words aloud. Until the last few weeks he'd had little interest in them. Things had *changed!*

With great care he lifted the booklet which was on top. Laying it aside, he took the second one out of the box. It had a big number two scratched on the cover. Folding the many pages of tablet paper several times, he pressed them down in the box, then put the top booklet back in place and closed the lid. If anyone opened the box it would look the same as always. It would seem funny reading the second diary first, but that was the way it would have to be.

Ed began to panic when he considered how he was going to re-lock the cabinet. Fortunately it proved to be quite simple. He pressed the locking pin back in the lock and carefully closed the door. He heard a satisfying "click" and the lock was closed again.

The boy stared at the forbidden pages with something like hunger. Now that he had volume number two, what was he going to do with it? It would have to be hidden, and hidden well, but where? Some place where his mom would never find it, but also where it would not suffer any sort of damage. "My satchel!" he thought. "No. Mom's always digging into my gym bag looking for dirty socks and stuff. No place in my room would be safe from her constant cleaning." Then it struck him. "My car! That's the perfect place. Neither Mom or Dad ever get into the Ford, at least not in the trunk, where I'll hide the thing until I'm done with it and can sneak it back into the cabinet!"

Getting dressed and going out to his car was out of the question for now. They would be coming home soon, and it wouldn't be wise to be caught outside when he was supposed to be sick in bed! He ran to the kitchen and opened the drawer where his mom saved used bread wrappers. There were a lot of them and certainly one wouldn't be missed. Still he pulled one from the bottom of the drawer and patted the rest down the way they'd been.

Back in the living room he picked up the little booklet and

wrapped it carefully in the bread wrapper. Just as he started to leave the room he saw it. The straightened safety pin lay in plain sight, right on top of the cabinet. He sucked in his breath, grabbed the pin, took a careful look around and headed for the stairs. He was in bed with the diary under his nightshirt when he heard the truck in the driveway.

X   X   X

The school bus was about half full when it stopped for him at the farm. It was a cold ride as usual, but the kids were used to it, their saying being, "the heater in this old thing only works in summer!" Jim, the bus driver, paid no attention to their complaints, as he had learned to completely ignore everything that went on behind him. Sometimes it was plenty!

Third period study hall finally arrived. Ed got permission to go to the library, where he settled himself at a little table in a back corner. There were other kids there, mostly girls, whose constant whispering earned them nasty looks from the library aide. With several textbooks stacked up to make a sort of shield, he started to open the bread wrapper. It made a crackling sound that sounded as loud as a gunshot.

"Ed Nolan!" Mrs. Moser hissed angrily. "There is to be no eating in this library! You know the rules!"

The boy shook his head violently, held up the waxed paper in one hand, and the diary in the other. Wise to such tricks, she stomped back to his table, settled her glasses on her nose and checked everything out. She even moved his American history aside to make sure no candy or other edibles were hidden there. Satisfied but still suspicious, she stalked back to her desk.

Almost reverently Ed lifted the battered cardboard cover. He'd had no chance to read it up to now. Chores, farm work, and his trap line had kept him busy, plus the fact that the necessary privacy was nearly impossible at home. The cover was no longer attached, the binding having disintegrated long ago, perhaps even while still in old Eli's possession.

The first line was a shock!

Oct 17, 1825 gess you could call this hyar buk number 2, sins I filed up one a them bufor stopt ritin in the first buk mam gimmee but haint rote fer a wile had nothing to say that's why. Ifn I gits caut wiuth thius hyar buk im likely to wake up feedin the fishees an a bowee nife stuk betwixt my ribs. Sum buddy needs to noe whats gwine on tho. So hyar goes

on this buk an it gots to be hid keerful ever day same as tother un.
Them was at it agin las nite L.C. an that othern the yunger 1 name a
J.W. I heered them leev the bunk hous must a bin bout 2 er so theys
gone most a the nite but I heered em come sneekin bak in jist bufor
sunup. Them wont be wurth salt in the wuds tuday an us needin to
snake out bout 12 big whites bufor sundown ile keep a eye on them 2
shur as shootin I will that. Today my birthday how bout that I tole
nobuddy caws im no greenhorn an iffen the rest a that there crue knoed
theyd throw me in the crick fer shore I seen that happen bufor an it's
not gwine to hapin to me no siree 20 yar tuday I am. Think it my tern to
do the horses so I beter git outn this hyar out hous an gitt to werk
Ginger and Tops reel gud werkers an easy to take keer of they don kik
ner bite and likes a gud curryin an that's a fackt. Ive seen them 2 hawl
out 8 big white pines in one lode an hardly no snow on the groun
neether Weuns all be sunk thout that thar teem fer shore. Bout them
horses Ginger an Tops I got my comuppens one time had it comin fer as
that's conserned wal them two culd warm up there shed most like a
stove an that's a fackt. 1 morning I give em a gud curryin an theys so
warm I jist kinda layed acrost ol Ginger she the biggest 1. rite over her
ol back I goes an first thang I jist soun asleep. Wal ol Avery he the boss
man snuk up on

me an dint do a thang but jabbed me in my stikin out reer end with a hay fork drawed blud too corse he hada tell all them otherns in are crue and them jist hollered an laffed they dern fuel heds off an that a fackt wal I had it comin ya culd say I rekon. Never done that thar agin an no misteak now Im outa hyar and to werk on my birthyday. Wonder what mam and pap is up to on this fine day in the fall purty in Ohiya now I bet its purty hyar to yeller red an ornge in them hardwoods glad we aint cutting them only white pines fer usns rite now enyways

"That was the bell Mr. Nolan!" Mrs. Moser snapped.

Ed gathered up his books, secured the diary in the bread wrapper and hurried to his next class. He had re-read the first entry several times, hardly bothered by the spelling and lack of punctuation. His mind was reeling from the mention of two of the young [at that time] man's bunk mates. They were certainly up to something, and Ed suspected that whatever it was might have something to do with the treasure.

With no more study periods that day, he had no time for further reading, but he heard little in his classes as old Eli's words replayed themselves over and over in his mind.

With the diary safely hidden under the jack in the car's trunk, he concentrated on doing an especially good job on his chores. After supper he brought up the subject he thought would be a hard sell.

"Now that basketball's over some of the guys are still driving to school," he began, trying to sound casual.

"That makes no sense," Calvin said. "Most of them had to drive then in order to stay for practice. I suppose you're wanting to keep on driving too, is that it?"

"Yeah, I do, but it's no big deal. If you say no it's o.k. . . ."

"I *am* saying no! If you're driving, it's hard to tell when you'll get home. I'll get stuck with your chores as well as mine. *No driving!*"

Ed swallowed his anger, knowing further argument would be futile anyway. He gathered his books and got ready to study.

"You still owe me eighty-five cents," Cal yelled after him. "Don't think I'll forget that!"

"I know it Dad. I haven't forgotten. After chores on Saturday morning I'm going to pull all my traps. I'll go over to Maysville and sell my furs. You'll get your money." His dad lowered the newspaper to see if any "smart alecky" talk was intended. Ed, his face deep in his math book, did not look up.

The moment passed.

CHAPTER THREE

The Treasure Map

J.R. REMICK, HIDES AND FURS. The hand-painted sign dwarfed the tiny building on the corner of highway nine and the main street of Maysville. Ed jumped out of his Ford and pushed the shed door open with his boot. Both his hands were full, as he was carrying three muskrats by their tails. He had been amazed to find two more animals when he pulled his traps that morning. The odor in the small building was very strong but the boy and Mr. Remick were both used to it.

"Eddie, Eddie! What you got for me today, boy?"

"Three. And all prime, corn-fed rats."

"Prime. Eh? Let's have a look." The man ran a practiced thumb and finger along the back legs of each small animal. "Two prime, one second", he announced.

Ed knew it was useless to argue, and the truth was that one of those he'd retrieved that morning was a little small, but he couldn't help himself. "How about six bucks?"

"Nope."

"Five eighty?"

"Nope. Five seventy-five kid."

J.R. counted out the money, which amounted to the agreed upon five dollars and seventy five cents. Ed couldn't believe his good luck. Even after paying his father there would still be four dollars and ninety cents for himself. The boy sat down on the only chair in the place to watch the fur buyer strip the hides. He was not really that interested in the skinning process, since he had seen J.R. do it hundreds of times, but ever since he had attempted to clean the barrel of the muzzle loader and encountered the obstruction, he had hoped that J.R. would be able to give him some help.

"Bought any guns lately?" Ed began.

"Went to a sale last Saturday. They had two, both cap and ball. Pretty nice shape."

"Did you get one?"

"Not a-tall! They went way too high for me. I got plenty of 'em anyway."

"How many you got now, J.R.?"

The man stopped skinning for a minute and gave Ed a suspicious look. "I got a few," was all he would say.

"I was just wondering. We've got one ourselves. Did I ever tell you that?"

"Only about twenty times," J.R. said, rinsing his hands in a bucket of pinkish water. He had skinned all three animals in less than five minutes. "Flint lock, right? Want to sell it?"

"No, it belongs to my mom, but maybe you could give me some advice. I was trying to clean the barrel the other day and I hit something that was stuck in there. Any ideas?"

"You shouldn't a tried to clean it *atall!* Collectors like to buy pieces that haven't been fooled with. Guess it don't matter none, since your mom prolly won't sell it anyway. Didn't damage the ramrod did you?"

"There wasn't any. The rod's been missing for as long as I can remember. Maybe my older brother, Calvin Junior, traded it off or something."

"What did you use on the barrel then?"

"Well," Ed answered sheepishly, "I took a thin dowel rod, cut a slot in the end, and stuck in a strip of old cloth. I soaked it with bore cleaner too."

Something that indicated agreement flickered in the fur buyer's eyes. "So you struck something, did you?"

"Yep, but whatever I hit was not all the way down. Maybe eight or ten inches from the lock."

"Prolly a ball. Could've come from a misfire or maybe too light a load. Could you move it at all?"

"Not at all. It was really tight. Is there any way to get it out? I mean short of trying to bust it up or something."

"What do you want it out of there for anyway? I spose it's something you'd like to carry around in your pocket to show the other boys. That it?"

"Boy, you've hit it right on the head," Ed replied. Lying seemed to be getting much easier!

"Well I guess I can understand that, seeing as how the gun is from some great, great, somebody or other in your ma's family. Come

In the house a minute."

The little house was quite clean and tidy, but there was no mistaking the lingering musky smell. J.R. entered a small room off the kitchen, closing the door behind him. Ed had no doubt that the man's gun collection was in that room, and that the fur buyer was particular about whom he allowed in there. He came out after a minute, carrying a long, thin wand of highly polished wood.

"This is what you need, kid," he said, holding it out. "In the end there is a little piece of a wood screw. Push this down on the ball and keep turning her. When it locks up, don't try to yank it back out. Run a little oil down the barrel and keep working it until you feel it loosen up. Take your time and out she'll come, slick as a whistle!"

"Boy, I really appreciate .. ."

"Just be sure that rod comes back to me as soon as you're done with it, and it better be in as good shape as it is now."

"I sure will! Thanks a lot for. . . ."

"Forget it. Just have that rod back to me in good order."

X   X   X

With the chores done and his twelve traps hung up in a corner of the milk house, Ed told his mom he was going hunting. He had paid his dad for the spilled milk, but still hadn't tried to remove the musket ball from the old flintlock rifle. Although he didn't want to admit it to himself, he was a little scared to use J.R.'s special tool. "If I broke that thing I don't know what would happen!" he thought. Going hunting was a good way to put it off for a while, but he vowed that when he got back he would get to work on it.

"How long will you be gone, Eddie?" his mom asked, watching him shrug into the hand-me-down game coat with the hunting license pinned on the back.

"Not long Mom. A couple hours maybe."

"You be careful, and don't go off our farm."

"I won't," he yelled, closing the door behind him. Boots on, he called the dog and they headed for the west pasture. Rabbits were almost always to be found in the high grass there, and it was open enough for clear shooting. Jiggs, a springer spaniel getting up in dog years, ranged ahead, working the timothy and swale, his nose to the ground.

Ed missed the first rabbit that burst from cover, but nailed the next two. "Two's enough to clean," he said, patting the old dog on the head. "Come on boy, we're heading for home. I'll have to dress out these critters and get to my chores. Good dog!"

With chores done and the rabbits skinned and soaking in salt water he hurried to the old log cabin they now called the "summer kitchen". A wood fire in the potbellied stove soon had the small room warming up. Seated once again on the old milk can, he held the gun between his knees, its stock resting on the floor. Gingerly he eased the rod down until its sharp, threaded point touched the ball. Almost holding his breath he applied light pressure and began turning. It seemed to be working! Suddenly it stopped. Ed dribbled a little light machine oil down the barrel and forced himself to wait several minutes. Carefully, very carefully, he worked the rod back and forth until suddenly it began to turn easily. He inched the rod upward a little at a time. He almost gave a victory yell when the heavily corroded bullet appeared at the muzzle. Then it was out!

Ed would forever thank his lucky stars for the action he now took. Grabbing up his home-made ramrod he inserted a dry patch and ran it up and down the barrel to blot up the small amount of oil that had not come out with the ball.

Shining his flashlight down the barrel, he let out a long, silent whistle. There was something down there for sure, and he was almost certain he knew what it was. He attached foot long piece of straight baling wire to the end of his ramrod. With trembling fingers he lowered it until it touched something at the end of the barrel. Twisting the wire did nothing. He withdrew the rod and wire, bent a tiny hook in the end and tried again. Something was coming up!

Forcing himself to be patient, he teased the rod upward until the wire showed. He stopped and shined the flashlight beam down along the wire. A piece of paper, brown and curled, was caught in the wire hook! Gently he eased it out, a tiny piece crumbling between his thumb and finger. A little oil showed along the edge. With the entire piece in his shaking hand, Ed laid it carefully on the work bench.

It was a _map!_

He was afraid to try to straighten it out, but finally could wait no longer. He unrolled it bit by bit, laying anything heavy he could grab on the edges to keep it flat. It was amazingly clear. Words, symbols and a few numbers jumped out at him. He wanted to shout, or dance, or sing.

He gave it a closer look. That it was a map there could be no doubt. It looked like an island or perhaps several islands, but what appeared to be the largest of them was only partly there! A ragged break slanted across the fragile paper, dissecting some words and numbers. As he examined the break where the map had parted he could see that the edge of the tear looked new. Hoping against hope, he shined the light down the barrel once more. There it was! The small missing section of the map was plastered against the inside of the barrel.

It was going to take much longer to peel that part away from the rusty metal. He thought he had it somewhat loose, when he heard heavy footsteps coming toward the summer kitchen door. He knew that step! He hardly had time to throw a rag over the map when the door burst open.

"You got any idea what *time* it is?"

"Oh boy!" he groaned. "Is it supper time already? Sorry Dad, I've been cleaning Mom's old gun and I guess I just didn't . . ."

"It's not supper time for *you* boy! Get your chores done then straight to your room! I'm going to break you of all your absentmindedness if it's the last thing I *do!* Take care of the stove, then get to the barn!"

"What do I care?" he exulted as his father's footsteps faded into the distance. "What's a missed meal compared to a genuine treasure map?" He was certain that was exactly what it was! Risking further wrath, he couldn't resist one more look before he hid the curling paper on a shelf behind some old canning jars. What was it that kept pulling his eyes to the very bottom of the old paper? "Oh *wow!* "He almost shouted. In the little word "after" which appeared near the bottom, he saw the letter F made the very same way as those in the diary! "Eli, you old rascal," he exulted, "this is *your map,* sure enough. Treasure, here I come!"

Chores finished, he picked up his school books and was heading for the stairs with no supper.

"You come here! You think I'm too tough on you don't you?" When Ed hesitated, his dad almost shouted. *"Answer me, boy!"*

"No, I don't think that. I know we did wrong, but that was three months ago for Pete's sake. Can't you ever forget. . ." Cal advanced on his son, arm raised to strike.

"Calvin!" Ed's mother hissed, lips compressed and eyes flashing.

"You go on up, Eddie, but no more talking back to your father."

School books and treasure map forgotten for the moment, he lay on his bed and listened to the wind whistling around the west corner of the house. He didn't want to think about what had happened three months ago, but he couldn't help it. The entire awful scene came back as if it had been only yesterday. . .

CHAPTER FOUR

Jail Birds

"Are you sure it's even there, Mike? When's the last time you saw it?"

"I'll say I'm sure! I was hauling manure for that old coot just last Saturday. I seen him dipping into that barrel a couple times that day."

"What if we get caught though?" Tom asked, chewing on a fingernail.

"Yeah, what if we get caught?" Eddie echoed. "My old man would knock the tar out of me, for sure!"

"*Nobody's* going to *get caught!*" Mike argued, coughing and choking. He'd started smoking, and was trying to learn to inhale. "Want a drag?" he asked. Neither of the boys took him up on it.

Ed was scared, but he certainly wasn't going to show it. "Why do you want to do it anyway?" he asked, eyeing the smoker. "It's just cider ain't it?"

"Hah!" Mike exploded, coughing some more. "That's all you know. Sure it's cider, HARD cider!"

"Does it really have a kick to it?" Tom asked.

"I'll say it does. See, here's how it works. Old man Kraus fills a barrel about half full of cider in the fall. In January he leaves it outside to freeze. The stuff freezes around the sides, but not in the middle, cause there it's almost pure alcohol. That's where you use your dipper."

"I wouldn't mind trying some of that stuff," Ed grinned.

"You'll get to. This Friday night!"

Tom was getting a little leery of the way the conversation was going. "No way, man. I've heard all about Jerrod Kraus. He hates kids. If he catches you it would mean getting clipped with a load of rock salt from his old twelve gauge."

"No, listen," Mike said earnestly. "I've got it all figured out. He always goes to have supper with his sister up in Wayland on Friday nights. He won't even be around. We can have ourselves a real time. Another thing. Hard cider don't have no smell to it neither." This was a complete lie, but the other two were impressed.

"I don't think I better, Mike. I've got a basketball game and a lot of homework. Better count me out."

"Eddie's a *scaredy cat! Eddie's a scaredy cat!*"

"I'll go, "Tom said.

"Look," Ed said in desperation, "if I go it will have to be late. The game's at home, but by the time I've showered up, I still couldn't get going before ten or so."

"Yeah, you better shower *real good,*" Mike laughed. "You must really work up a sweat settin' the bench like you always do. O.K., I'll pick you both up after the game outside the south locker room door. See ya."

Two days later all three found themselves crammed into the cab of Mike's dad's pickup. He drove on by the Krause farm once. Not a light was showing. "Told ya!" the ring leader gloated. He swung the truck around in the middle of the road and gunned it back to Krause's driveway.

"What will we use for a dipper?" Tom asked, elbowing Ed in the side.

"Won't need none."

"Why not?" Ed asked. "We gonna dip it out with our hands?"

"Won't need a dipper because we're taking the *whole thing!*"

The other two boys began to object violently, but Mike swung the truck right up to the back door of a machine shed. "Come on. It's late! Let's get this thing loaded and get out of here before old 'shingle sides' shows up!"

Confident that no one was at home, they made no effort to be silent. The door was unlocked but no one had thought to bring a flashlight. They stumbled around until Tom bumped into it. Half carrying and half sliding the surprisingly heavy barrel, they finally made it out the door.

"What you gonna do with this thing when you get it home?" Ed asked, tugging at their unwieldy burden.

"I'm hiding it back of the hay bales in our barn. By the time we use up all the hay, this old barrel will be empty, and I'll burn it."

It was a real struggle lifting it into the truck bed, but they did it. All three were laughing, punching each other, and acting kind of crazy.

Suddenly a bright light came on from a pole beside the shed. Apparently Mr. Krause had either got back early or he had not gone to Wayland after all!

"What's going on out there?" he yelled. "Get out of that truck *right now* or I'll shoot!" A glint of light shining off his shotgun barrel proved he was not kidding!

"Let's *go!*" Mike yelled. He pushed the accelerator down hard, and they were heading out. With no time to shut the tailgate, the barrel slid out, hit the ground, and smashed to pieces. There was a tremendous **bang!** It seemed that almost at the same moment the truck lurched sideways and stopped, the left front tire blown to pieces from a load of buckshot.

"Get down out of there! I still got one barrel left! Now you all get in the house. No funny stuff, 'cause I got every right to shoot you for the theft of my property."

He made them sit on the kitchen floor while he kept the huge old scatter gun trained on them.

"Take off your shoes!" he snarled. They did so, glancing at each other in fear.

"Now your *pants!*"

"Hey, what is this?" Mike asked sullenly.

"You shut your mouth, Mike! So this is how you treat a man who pays you good wages for easy work?"

Mike wanted to retort, but he was not totally stupid. They took off their pants. The man kicked their clothes into a corner, telling them not to move. Keeping one eye on his prisoners he quickly called the sheriff. The boys sat there looking ridiculous in coats and hats but no trousers.

Their parents were called, but despite some pleading, all three spent the night and the next day in jail.

Nothing could have been worse!

X   X   X

He almost wished he could bawl, but lying there with his eyes closed he had relived every moment of the shame and pain he'd caused, not only for himself but even more so for his mom and dad. His mother had been just as angry and humiliated as her husband, but still she had managed to keep Cal from giving Ed the beating he really deserved. It was also she who'd kept the secret from Calvin Junior, Ed's older brother, who was recently discharged from the navy.

"Enough of this," Ed told himself silently. "It's all over now, or would be if he could just forget it." Then he had a thought. Knowing that as part of his punishment his parents would not enter his room until morning, he soon figured a way to get the diary.

"Mom," he yelled, "I've got to drain the radiator in my car. It's supposed to be down around zero tonight and I don't think I've got enough anti-freeze in it."

"What?"

He repeated his request. Lying was almost getting to be a habit!

"If you have to, go ahead I guess. Your dad is in the shop, welding, so if you're careful maybe he won't see you. If you get caught there's nothing I can do to help you." She did not offer him any supper.

Never had he been more careful. With not even a flashlight, he sneaked out to the corn crib. He always parked his car beside it where it was somewhat out of the wind. Feeling around in the trunk, he soon encountered the tire jack and the cellophane-wrapped diary beneath it. With the manuscript inside his shirt he ran up the stairs to his bedroom. He'd made it!

He began to read. Many brief entries were quickly scanned. They were interesting enough, but not what he was hoping to see. On several battered pages there was just a series of dates in the months of September and October, 1825, with little more than weather conditions noted. Then came a page which caught his attention right away.

Novembur 1 – 1825 this bin quite a day fust off the new kid Billy near cut his toe offn but kep on goin big as enythang he a reel peece a werk. He come on are crue bout a month ago hardly knoed which end was the ax hed but weuns liked him rite off he a hard werker ya culd say heed do enythang fer enybuddy even if he warnt no gud at nothing. The boss gives himn hale columbya alla time but usns does sum of the werk fer him when the boss not lookin he gots a wife an little kid but never sez whar they are at. He gots a little pitcher of his woomin that he carrys aroun alla time he woulnt quit a werkin even wen his toe got bad cut sed he needed the monee to send her and the baby. We all of usns like him and tried to help out but he wouldn niver tell his last name. Billy is all he sed. Whatever bad stuf goin on I thinkd the boss man in on it like taday we was reely cutting timbre laffin an Billy gimpin aroun on his bad cut foot when Avery the boss man sez we needs to dubble teem to git the logs out. Whys that I thinks to meself thars plenny a new snow and Ginger an Tops is pulin fine an dint need no help as I kin see ennyways. Avery sez hes goin to Bear Crossing and rent a pair to help Ginger an Tops which like I sed we don need no extry pair then he ups ans sez Lewis an Wade was to go long why do you need three giys to dryve a teem which we don need enyyways back to the cutting area? We was all usns wondrin the same too the boss man he puts Henry in charg as straw boss boy we was glad of that there soons Avery an them other 2 was gone wed have ourselves som fun and we did thats shore Mickee had sum bakin and I had bread so we bilt usns a fire an had usns some brekfus ha ha. Like I sed we dint do much werk tuday not with the boss man an his toadies gone to rent them horses we dint need ennyway that thar bakin shor hit the spot the snow was hevy an we was still abel to have 13 whites loded up an reddy to hawl out when him an them comeback with2 mitey nice draft horses to help Ginger an Tops which they dint need as I sed bufor. Them 3 was up to som thang ir my name aint Eli Yoder they dint do hardlee no werk till evenin when they gots back hyar they dint talk to no buddy but thereselves but that be how they air alla time ennyway. Avery was ritin in a little book he gots but he kep it outa site mostly. I gits up to go to the privy an jist werked it sos I culd go rite past him an his little book open on the table. Hed rote some numbers down an they shor dint look like timber numbers to me

I only gots a quik look but I seen he had dates ritten an beside them dates he put down like 2 cases er 1 case ect. He give me a look so I gots outa thar fast but I seen what I seen what the heck cases of what Im wondrin.

Ed closed the diary and sealed it up in the bread wrapper. He had to shake his head a little to bring himself back to the Ohio farm. Despite Eli's lack of correct spelling and almost no punctuation, the journal had taken him back over a hundred years to a logging crew in the forests of northern Michigan. "What a story," he thought as he slipped the little book under his pillow. "Man it looks like he was taking a real chance by writing all that down. I imagine back in those days if he'd been caught there would have been a bad 'accident' in the woods!"

"Wonder what was in those cases, Ed was thinking. "It must be something really valuable. Maybe that's what the treasure is. And maybe the map was made to show where it's hidden!"

He was awake for two hours, partly because he was hungry, but mostly due to excitement.

School was held up the next morning. Drifting snow had closed nearly all of the country roads, but the plows had been out all night, so the school buses were making their rounds after the two hour delay.

Chores done, Ed had the biggest breakfast he could remember. His mom smiled a little but didn't let Cal see it. Eggs and sausage disappeared rapidly as the teenager made up for his unwelcome fast the night before. "Why are you taking your gym bag?" she asked, watching him get ready for the bus.

"I've got three books and my school shoes to carry," he said, failing to mention that Eli's diary was hidden at the bottom of the bag.

"I hope you put your old shoes in a paper bag or something!"

"Yeah, I did Mom. I sure wouldn't want to get these wonderful school books dirty or anything." The sarcasm was very apparent.

Cal looked up from his plate, a serious eye on his son. "Does your car have enough anti-freeze in it? It's supposed to get down below zero again tonight. That car is your responsibility remember."

"Yeah, it's fine. I put a whole gallon in it last Saturday. That 'stop-leak' you gave me really works too. The radiator doesn't even drip anymore."

His mother caught his eye and gave him a questioning look. "What was he doing out at his car last night if he knew it had plenty of anti-freeze?" she wondered. She and her son would need to have a serious talk, and it had better be soon.

Ed's mind was certainly not on his school work that day. He did manage to look interested as his teachers did their best to motivate the kids, but they had a real challenge. It was snowing again and the wind was coming up. Not only the students, but the teachers as well were hoping for a day off. Or at least another late start.

Ed was wracking his brain trying to think up a viable excuse to spend a couple hours in the summer kitchen. He needed more time to make a second attempt to free the remaining piece of the map. "I can't say I need to clean the muzzle loader *again.* Nobody would believe that!" he thought, rubbing his chin. "Maybe I should just tell Mom and Dad the whole story; the diary, the map, all of it." But in his heart he knew that he would never do that unless forced into it. He hardly admitted to himself the reason for such secrecy. Why not let them know all that he was finding out? Because if the map made sense he intended to go after the treasure, and after his brush with the law they would never allow it! He vowed to keep his mouth shut and keep things the way they were.

Miracles do happen! When Ed had finished chores and supper was over, his mom had a request. "Eddie, would you go out to the summer kitchen and bring me about a dozen of the pint-sized mason jars? Ladies Aid is meeting here tomorrow night and I want to give each of them a jar of my blackberry jam."

"Sure, Mom," Eddie said, a little too quickly, he was afraid. "Tell you what. Some of those jars might be cracked, and all of them are really dusty. If you'll put some water and soap chips in the old wash pan I'll heat it up on the stove out there. I'll need a couple clean cloths too. I'll check them over, clean them up, and have them ready for your 'hen party'." This was not a lie at all. He really did mean to clean the jars, but he would do it fast in order to have some time to do some "fishing" for the map fragment. "I'll go out and start a fire so I don't freeze out there. Be back in a little while to get the stuff to clean them with."

She was not only somewhat amazed at this sudden desire to help, but was more than a little suspicious. She decided to pay him a little visit after a while. *"I'll bet he's smoking out there,"* she gasped. "If he is, there's no way he can hide the smell from me. Yes, I'll just drop in on that son of mine!"

Ed had an idea that his mom was not fooled. He shouldn't have acted so eager. Precautions were called for! The jars were not very dirty at all. Stored upside down on the shelf, they only had collected a little dust. He counted out twelve, wiped them off fast, and rolled each one in the warm water. He did not dry them yet. "If she comes out here, I'll be drying them then."

He took a thirteenth jar down and began tapping it around the top with a screwdriver. In only a few minutes a small crack appeared along the rim. Grinning, he set it out, away from the others.

He made sure that the first part of the map was still well hidden on a high top shelf. The gun was so cold it nearly froze his fingers as he handled it, since the small building had not been heated for several days. He had returned the fur buyer's tool, but his home-made one was what he needed now anyway.

Seated on his favorite old milk can, he began what he was calling the "fishing" attempt. It was not easy. Apparently the missing map fragment had bonded with the rifle barrel. Ed tried everything, twisting and turning the wire every which way, but finally, as sometimes happens, when he was about to give up, the hook snagged a loose section of the parchment. Excitement growing, he very gently began to draw it out. When a ragged edge appeared at the muzzle he seized it between a finger and thumb and pulled.

It was obvious at once that he had not been able to get it all. The newest section, about the size of his palm, showed writing and some numbers he didn't understand at all. He was in the act of retrieving the main part of the map when he heard his mom's footsteps crunching through the snow. He jammed the precious piece of paper inside his jacket. As the door opened he was busily drying a jar.

"Are you about done with them? I didn't think it would take you this long. I could have washed them inside anyway." She picked up a jar and turned it over in her hands. "Looks like I'll *have to* wash them again inside. These aren't very clean!"

"I got the worst dirt off, Mom. This one's cracked, see?"

For a long moment Beth looked at the flintlock, which was still standing by the work bench. Her eyes then flicked back at her son. "So you got the bullet out of the barrel did you?"

"Yep. J.R. loaned me a tool to use. Want to see the ball?" He fished it out of his pocket and handed it to her.

"It's white," she said, surprised. "Is it lead? All the lead I ever saw was black."

"That's what I thought too, Mom. I showed it to J. R. and he said that lead turns white when it gets old. According to him it's the way that kind of metal oxidizes, like when iron rusts. I been carrying it in my pocket for a good luck piece."

"Well don't you lose that thing . Better let me put it up somewhere or it'll be gone. Now I'll help you get these jars inside. Come on, I'm cold."

"You go ahead Mom. I need to bank the fire first. Don't want to burn the old summer kitchen down!"

She left, arms full of jars. He quickly cleared off the high shelf and retrieved the map. Breathlessly he spread it out on the work bench, using hand tools to hold the curling edges. The new piece fitted precisely into the upper right hand corner. Moving the fragment around, he was suddenly shocked when a crack appeared through the center of the larger piece. It didn't come completely apart, but he could see that when he rolled it up again it would undoubtedly split.

Ed knew what must be done. He slipped both pieces under his sweater, put on his coat and left the little building. At the first chance he got he'd have to make a copy of the map, before it fell completely apart. "By golly!" he thought as he headed up the steps, "I know just the guy to do it! Tom's a pretty good artist. I'll bet he could make a fairly good copy. Then I can hide the real map in the summer kitchen again."

CHAPTER FIVE

Accomplice

Ed was seated at a long table in the high school library. He kept his library pass in plain sight, in case the monitor might want to make sure he had one. The diary lay open in front of him, its bread wrapper cover stuffed in his book bag. He began to read at the entry dated November 12th, 1825.

We had a man kilt tuday. No buddys fawlt the tree twisted on im jist wenj it started to fall wal sir it kiked bak and jist cawt him rite in his midel he never bleeded much not much as youd notic anyhow we layed im out as best we culd then we was bak to loggin agin jist like bufor. That nite we tuk im to a sawbones in Bear Crossing sed hed take keer a him. He had fokes down in Tenessee er somwhars we herd he was a good werker an it was jist a acciden his name was elmer but weuns called him red he dint mind that he sed. Avery an them 2 is at it agin how many did you git the boss man asts one a them he sed he gots only 1 case. cases of what I wanted to know but they wasn sayin nothing but then I was feered to ast whats goin on. Mind yer own bidness papa allus sed or youl likely git in trubel fer shor. That's jist what I done you bet but Id shor Ike to know what theys up to all bout them cases an all see. Wen weuns got bak from takin Red to the dokter in Bear Crossing the boss ol Avery he sez come on in the bunk house all a youuns so we did. Were gittin to bout a ship lode any day now he sez so I gon to be gon fer a cupla days to see bout gittin a ship. Were hedin fer Shicawga with our timber an gon to need 4 mens to go along LC an JWs goin so need 2 more hows about you Eli an billy to. We both sed wed go so now we gots to werk like the dikens to fill the lode so the bote kin go afor freeze-up. Avery tryin to git one a them newfangled paddle wheelers hope he can git it caws it prolly make fer a fast passage I hope. In this hyar litel book I use letters LC an JW so ifn I gets cawt they'll not know who I bin talkin about purty smart aint I?

"What's so funny?" Jane asked, plopping her books down next to his. She thought she was Ed's girlfriend but he wasn't so sure about that.

"Reading in this old diary that was handed down to my mom," he grinned. "Here, take a look. Easy! *Easy,* girl! The pages are about to fall apart. You have to be real gentle with them. Also, Mom doesn't know I've got this book. If something would happen to it I'd probably be grounded for *life!*"

"How can you read this stuff? He can't spell hardly at all, and you can't tell where one sentence stops and another one begins. This would drive me nuts!"

"You do get used to it pretty quickly. Tell you what. I'll read some of it to you next . . ."

"Jane! Back to your seat. No talking, you two."

That ended their conversation, but seventh period was about over anyway.

X   X   X

"Where'd you get this thing?" Tom asked, gingerly handling the crackling document. "Is it real? Oh, I get it. You made this up *yourself* didn't you? Where'd you get the old paper to draw it on? A nice touch! Looks like the inside lining of a wheat seed bag. That it?"

"Listen, Tom, this thing is *real!* I found it in the barrel of my great, great grandpa's flintlock rifle."

"What a story!" Tom laughed. "I could almost believe you, but I know you too well."

"Listen, friend, would I lie to you? After all we were jailbirds together, right? I tell you it's true. Don't you remember seeing that old gun in our summer kitchen? You know, where I work on my traps and stuff."

"Sure, I remember seeing it there. It's a neat old gun, but . . ."

"But *nothing!* I was trying to clean the barrel and I hit a lead ball stuck in there. I fished it out and this map was in the barrel behind it. Here's the bullet." Ed pulled the ball from his pocket. Showing his friend the hole where the screw had gone in did the trick. Tom was beginning to think that maybe it could be true. They were sitting in Ed's car after school. He'd been given permission to drive to school because there was a meeting of his journalism club. The heater didn't work, so they didn't talk long.

"You know Ed this could be a map to show where something valuable was stashed. Like a. .a . . *treasure map!*"

"Tom, old buddy, I'm going to tell you some stuff, but you've got to swear to me you'll not tell a*nybody!*"

"Sure. What's the story?"

"I meant it about swearing not to tell. Give me your hand."

"What *is* this? You're acting kind of *weird!*"

"Not a word until you promise not to tell *anybody.*"

"O. K., I swear not to tell, but I think you're going nuts."

Ed began at the beginning, telling the whole story just as it had happened up to that day. Tom was impressed.

"You mean even your mom and dad don't know? You're heading for trouble! My folks are still mad about 'the great cider robbery'. I wouldn't want to do anything that would make things worse," Tom said.

"Me either. That's why they don't know, and why you have to keep your trap shut about this. Get it?"

"O.K., O.K. I'll make you a real nice copy. I've got some good paper I use in art class. Think that will be o.k.?"

"That'll be swell. How soon can you get it done?"

"Tomorrow night. My folks will just think I'm working on a project for art class. This is gonna cost you, you know."

"How much?"

"Let's say five bucks."

"Let's *don't* say that. How about two?"

"Two fifty, O.K.?"

"Tom you ought to be selling used cars, but o.k. two fifty, but be sure you have the original back to me tomorrow for sure. Keep it closed up in this envelope, and be real careful with it. It's falling apart. If anything breaks off, be sure to save all the pieces."

"You got it."

"And one more thing. See these numbers and lines and little symbols? Be sure you include them in the copy, and as close as you can to exactly where they are on the original, all right?"

"I should have held out for more dough," Tom sighed.

Ed was not at all sure he had done the right thing. His friend was trustworthy enough, but it was scary to have another person in on the secret, good buddy or not!

11.16.25 Looks like he gots one lined up it's a new shIp too he clames shes like the Savannie that crost the oshun in 1819. That was some ship all rite if ourns as good we uns be in Shicago town in a hury you bet. She gots side wheelers on her an a 2 master so sail er steem don make no differns. Cant see why Avery in sich a allfard hurry fer we culd git to Shicago uner sail easy an no wood ner cole to burn nor pay fer neither Well its hisn to do with I say. Him an them 2 of hisn gone a lot an some times they not back the same day They allus talkin and lurkin about but not cutting no timber so how are the rest of usns sposed to fill the order werkin short handed like we are now I guess we git it done some how. Ice in the inside water bucket this morning so better git to loggin. Freeze –up comin purty soon an no misteak. This hyar ritin 4 days latern that other. We got all cut fer a full lode an down to the river. We gots rafters to help usns they shore know how to make timber go on down the river never seen the like of it. Billy an me to go on down to the port an help lode timber on that there side-wheeler in 2 days the ship named Caroline. She a buety an looks fast to me I don't like steem culd blow up er somthin but no buddy asts me what I wanted will be somthin ridin on that there new-fangled thang. I not know nothing about sail spose I gon to learn soon enuf ha ha. Here comes the boss man an them other 2 with him they gonna drive the new team an wagon down to the port now why wuld they do that an me an Billy have to go on a flatboat down thar. Shor but that was some ride down the Driggs Rivre on that flat boat no werk fer a day an a haf an grub purty good too me an Billy jist set an watched the woods role by. Onst I seen a deer a big doe it were she was jist standin and lookin at usns an I grabbed ol Betsy an drawed a beed on her but the flatboat guy sez you shoot that thar deer an youl swim fer it cuz we aint stopping fer nothing not on this trip even wen we hits the Manistick River rite down close to Manistick town no siree he sez. I culda took her easy we was movin slow like an the deer wasn't movin atall. Ol Betsy woulda done her fer sure an weuns aint had no venison fer a cunes age but no means no an I dint want to do no swimming in that thar cold river no sir I dint so we et beans an sow belly like always but no werk an that's a good thang.

Whys all this goin on I sez to Billy and he sez why too we don't know and don't ast nothing keepin our ol noses clean like daddy tol me wen Is a young'un ha ha. Seems purty late start down thar to Shicaga they say storms kin still be big on Mishigan Lake in december hope we don't run into any but Avery sez shut up an help lode so we does that. Course Avery an them 2 gots thar to the port bufor weuns did them goin in the wagon they shor in a awful herry to git them big pines loded an git *goin he sez snap it up boys but weins kin only lode one timber at a time on the winch so we do alls we kin do. Spose to git away in 2 days I think that make it Dec. 1 hope so don't like the looks a thangs on the wether. Storm acomin I thinkin gots wood an cole on board fer the boiler.*

gots to git goin an I begin to see why Avery in such a bother but wether aint all of it I thinks an Billy thinks so too. The boss sez keerful of the loadin don't drop the timber he sez How kin you hurt pine logs I wonder an Billy does too. Thers somthin down under them big pine logs is my thinkin yessir down there in the hold.

X   X   x

"Mr. Ivers," Jane Wilkins had a hand raised and waited until the American history teacher nodded. "You ought to see the old diary that Ed's grandpa or somebody wrote. It's really *nifty!*"

"Really? What about that, Ed? Something your grandfather left to your family?"

"Uh . . .no . . .it's not much really. His spelling was so bad you can hardly read it."

"Worse than yours?" someone whispered. The class laughed but Mr. Ivers wasn't through yet.

"Why don't you bring it in? It's real history after all. Must date from the late eighteen sixties or so, right?"

"Actually," Ed could not help saying, "it's from my great, great grandpa, dated in the eighteen twenties, but I can't bring it to class. It belongs to my mom and it's almost falling apart. She'd never want it passed around and everything. Sorry."

"That's o.k. We wouldn't want anything to happen to something so valuable, at least to your family, as a diary that old would be. Robert, we'll hear your report now."

After class Tom caught up with him in the hall. "Looks like *somebody* let the cat out of the bag," he laughed. "You shouldn't have showed it to Jane, she's got the biggest mouth in school."

"I couldn't help it. She saw me reading it in the library so I was caught. You haven't told anybody have you?"

There was a long pause. *Too long!* "Well, not *hardly* anybody . . that Darrel Stites, he just dragged it out of me."

"Thanks good friend! So much for taking an oath and everything. If Mom or Dad hears about it I'll be grounded for a long time. *If* that's all they do to me."

At supper two days later, Beth brought up the subject of the P.T.A. meeting which would be held at school the next night. "Why don't you go too, Cal? They never last long, and they usually have refreshments. Lots of Dads go. Sarah and Clyde always go. We could sit with them. How about it? I hate to always go alone."

"Got too much to do. Sorry. I need to finish the weld on the wagon axel. We're going to need feed and I don't trust the wagon unless I get a better weld on that crack. Besides, 'refreshments?' Cookies and punch I suppose! No, I don't intend to go. Ed could take you if you're afraid to drive."

"I'm not afraid, but it's for *both* Moms and Dads. I really wish you'd make an effort to attend, Cal."

"P.T.A. stands for 'parent' teachers association. Just 'parent', not parents with an s. One parent should be enough. That's all I've got to say about it."

Ed had heard the exchange and was hoping they would both be gone so he could read some more from the diary. He was anxious to get through it so he could exchange this second journal with the first one, finish that one, and get them both safely back in the cabinet. There was no arguing with this father, however. Even Beth couldn't make him budge once he'd made up his mind. "Maybe Dad will be working in the shop tomorrow night. That would give me a chance to get some things done while I'm alone," he thought.

Like many plans carefully made, it was not to be. Ed was needed in the shop to help his dad with the wagon repair. Beth got home just as the boy and his father were washing up. When asked how the meeting went, she hardly said a word about it. She looked angry! Both men assumed she was still upset about attending the meeting alone. That was not it. *Not at all!*

"Eddie, would you come down to the basement a minute? I need help getting some preserves out of the fruit room." She stomped down the stairs, Ed following along.

She yanked the sliding door open, turned on the light, and closed the door after them. "You are in *big trouble,* my boy! If your father finds out about this I can't be responsible for what could happen. I'm so *mad . . . I'm . . .I'm. . ."*

"Mom, what's wrong? What did I do? What about Dad finding something out? What *is this?"*

She grabbed his cheek with one hand, the way she used to do when he was little. "Don't give me that!" she hissed. "I'll tell you what you did. Jane Wilkins' mother was at the meeting tonight. As we were walking out, she said how wonderful it must be to have my great grandpa's hand-written journal. Her daughter had read some of it at school!"

"But Mom, I can . . . ."

"But *nothing!* You listen to me. You were absolutely forbidden to touch those journals and you know it. Also, now I know how there came to be a crack in the glass door of the cabinet. You *liar!* You not only did what was forbidden, you even broke into my locked cabinet. As I said, if your father knew about this there would be real punishment, so for now at least, I won't tell him. The next time you and I are alone I expect a complete and truthful explanation. There will be consequences, but that is to be determined." She grabbed two jars of fruit from the shelf without even looking at them. She shoved them into his hands, selected two for herself, and followed him out of the basement fruit room.

The following evening while Cal was falling asleep in his favorite chair, she announced her son's punishment.

Motioning Ed to the kitchen, she began. "Where is Eli's diary right now?" He dug it out of his book bag and held it out. It was still in the bread wrapper. "You are to copy every page of this diary. *Every page!* You are to copy it word for word with Eli's spelling and punctuation. When you finish this one, you will also do the other one, which I understand is Eli's first one. Use your own money to buy two good quality notebooks, one for each diary. Do you understand?"

Ed did his best to appear angry and sullen at such punishment, but secretly he could not have imagined anything he would *rather* do. "All right, I'll do it, but it's going to take some time."

"There's one more thing."

He stared at her, waiting for the bomb she was about to drop. "Your car is completely *off limits.* You will not drive it anywhere without my permission. Also, if by your attitude or demeanor you allow your father to become suspicious of your new stay-at-home policy I will tell him every detail of your lying, your theft of my property, and the breaking into of my locked cabinet. Is that also clear?"

"Yes, Mom. I'm really sorry. I'll never do anything like this again. You can trust me."

It would not be until nearly five years later, when he was fighting in the Korean War, that Ed finally realized that the "punishment" she meted out to her then sixteen-year-old was no punishment at all. It had actually protected him from the wrath of his father, assured the preservation of the fragile diaries, and allowed him the freedom to continue delving into the fascinating written records of a time long past. She was quite a mother!

12.4.25 Been holed up hyar 3 days weuns got all a her loded an reddy to sail or steem I shuld say I gess. wether is terrible Avery sez we wait til calm but he shor wantin to git started south on the big lake hoppin on 1 foot then tother he that wantin to go. Hes funy to watch all narvus like but Billy an me we don't let the boss man see usns laffin at him no sirree we shor don't do that. Billy sez the seegulls gots more sense than weuns does see he sez they stay over the land where its safe when a storm comin we shuld do the very same Billy sez but that not goin to happen Im thinkin. Wind got around to westerly an Avery sez we go so here we air out on the big lake that's some water I tell you the wind down some but still big waves. J W. sick an throwin up over the rail Avery makin fun of him want some greesy pork chops he asts him that makes the poor guy sickern ever so Avery laffs his head off. Me an Billy we keeps our traps shut but it's a meen trick fer shor funny or not. This hyar water gittin ruffer alla time I may be a litell sick my own self but not like J.W. so far. That steem ingin somthin fer shor she makes lotsa smoke an is noisy but we haint hardly needed no sails not yet anyways theres three sailers abord the Caroline they knows there bidness Billy an me don't have hardly no werk them salers an Big Lars hes the captin an a good one too thems the ones knows what has to be done. We help out when we kin but mosly jes stay outn the way Billys bettern me he sez he werked on a sailbote onct an it shor shows the salers likes him fer it they don't take to me much which sutes me fine less werk fer me I sez.

12.5.25 well so much fer them padel wheels I sez to Billy he jist laffed an shook his red head caws he thought the same as I do. Them padel wheels barkin an groanin like a sick dawg ha ha stick to sail Billy sez but Avery herd that an near nocked Billy rite down on that little door hatch I think they calls it but Billy he keeps his trap shut so do I after that I don't want to git nocked down like he done. Captin sez we go back to port shaft bent so only way to fix her is a blacksmithy. Avery maddern a wet hen he dont no way want to go back in but that's what the Captin sez were doin anyways.

12.6.25 Took her apart I helped an Billy too we gots the bent peece onto the land an a smithy heeted her an got her back in shape I allus thot Id be a smith some day but hyar I am waitin an goin on a bote to Shicago who can figger thangs? Misterius ways like they sez. Too late in the yar to be goin on the big lake but Avery is rarin to go so spose weuns will try agin hoipe no storms this time but prolly will be though

12.7.25 purt near lost my good frend Billy this day wind was reel bad all nite them padel wheels throwin spray all over the bote an it freezing on riggin an stays. Billy was hawlin sail with them salers hes good to help an knows his bidness lost his footin on the icy floor I mean deck an rite on over the side well youd not bleeve whats next no sir even I culdnt bleeve it my own self. Avery jist jumped rite in a grabed Billy hes not very big Billy aint an jist took him by the coller an held him up from gittin drownded the Captin jist reversed them padel wheels an the Caroline bcked up purty as pie so weuns culd drag them 2 abord. I throwed a line an drug them in. Couldn a done that with only sails no siree They was both good no siknes but moren middlin cold I tell you. Billy fine now Avery too Avery not so bad mebbe Im thinkin but you never seen J.W. ner L.C. do nothing I noticed.

CHAPTER SIX

Big Brother

"Are they really going to make it home this time do you think?"

Ed and his parents were finishing breakfast on a cold April morning. "Well they sure are planning on it," Beth replied, refilling Cal's coffee cup. "It's hard for him to get away from that offshore drilling rig. His letters say they've got him working six days and sometimes even seven days a week."

"I wonder how much that kid makes these days," Cal mused. "Must be mighty good wages! He's certainly earned it though. A navy 'frogman' is dangerous duty. We can be glad he never told us much of what he was doing on those landings during the war. You'd have been worried to death!"

"So would *you* have been Cal! I can't wait to see them again. The baby must be crawling by now. Jenny is so pretty and a good mother too. Seems like the days are just dragging by, but Saturday's coming. It's going to be *so nice!*"

Ed grabbed a piece of cold toast and washed it down with a glass of milk. "Junior probably don't even remember me anymore. Overseas almost four years, then living down there in Louisiana. The truth is I don't know him very well either."

"This will be a good visit. You two can spend some time together over your Easter break from school, but now Eddie you'll have to be careful about what you ask him about the war. He might not want to talk about that. It must have been terrible."

"Aw, Mom, I'm not totally stupid you know."

"Ed!" his dad said, rising from the table. "Watch your mouth!"

"What did I say?" Ed snapped, his temper rising. "I didn't mean that as 'back talk', did I Mom?"

"Let's not spoil the moment," she pleaded. We'll just look forward to seeing our son and his family again, O.K.?"

X   X   X

"How do you like living in Louisiana, Junior? Not much like Ohio, I'll bet."

"It sure isn't," his older brother answered. They were sitting on boxes in the old summer kitchen, finally away from the noise and confusion in the house. In addition to Ed's older brother and his family there were two uncles, an aunt, and several cousins for the Easter meal. Two babies, one of them Junior's, were crying and all the women were fussing over them. "Yep, Louisiana's not like Ohio at all. For one thing, it's hot almost all the time. And it's *muggy!*"

"Well you know it gets pretty sticky here in Ohio too," Ed grinned. "So how's your job going? Your letters said they had you working a lot of overtime."

"That's right, but I'm glad of it. Jenny and I are saving up to buy a house as soon as we can, so I'm down under as often as they'll let me."

"Diving, you mean?"

"Yeah, just like I did in the navy, only now nobody's shooting at me, thank God!"

"Do you go down alone? Does somebody on the surface keep your air coming? Man that must be scary! Got sharks down there?"

"Our company, 'Deep Water Enterprises', has a rule that nobody goes down alone. That's one rule I'm glad about. No sharks that I've seen. Not yet anyway! We don't need a tender on the ship. We got our own air in tanks on our backs. We can go about anywhere down below.

"You know I think I read about that kind of diving in Science Today magazine a couple years ago. Some French guy figured out how to do it I think."

"We learned all about that in dive school. They called us 'Frogmen'. The navy trained me real well, and that's how I landed my job. A lot of ex-service men and women aren't so lucky. They're having trouble finding work. Enough work talk. Mom tells me you've been reading some old diaries. She must have got them from Grandma when Grandpa died. I was in the service then. I'd like to read them too, but probably won't have time this trip."

"They're really neat. That is if you can read his writing. Man I thought I was a bad speller! Tell you what. I'm copying them off right now. I'll mail you copies when I've finished the job. About those diaries . . . I never told Mom or Dad, but I found something in the barrel of the muzzle loader." He nodded at the gun hanging on the wall behind the stove.

"Found a lot of rust I'd guess," Junior grinned, his gold tooth gleaming in the light.

"You won't tell them will you? If I tell you what was in there?"

"Well, I won't tell unless it's money or maybe some kind of dope," he laughed.

"Listen, Junior, it's a *map!* I think it's a *treasure map!*"

"Sure it is! Probably drawn up by Captain Kidd himself! Or better yet, somebody in the family stuck it in there as a practical joke. You know better than to believe in treasure maps don't you? What are you thinking?"

"Nobody 'stuck it in there' as you put it, because it was hidden behind an oversized lead ball. I had one heck of a time getting the bullet out. Here it is." He fished it out of his pocket and handed it over, explaining the tool the fur buyer had loaned him.

"So the old guy's still skinning 'rats, is he? I sold a bunch of them to him when I was a kid. So this hunk of lead was jammed down in there was it?"

"It sure was, and so tight it must have kept the map from getting wet or anything. There's probably another bullet right up by the breech. Between the two, old Eli had a safe place to hide the map once he was done using the gun for hunting. Want to see the map? Remember, not a word to Mom or Dad." Junior was laughing as his brother brought it down from the shelf.

Calvin Junior was suddenly impressed. "It really does look old all right. What happened to the corner?"

"I couldn't get all of that piece out. It went all to pieces. There wasn't enough left to fit in the missing part."

"This is an island he's showing." Junior's early skepticism was completely gone. "See these numbers and symbols? He's showing depths and shoals. We had a little map reading in the navy. I could tell you what most of the notations mean, but I don't want to write on this document."

"I've got a *copy!*"

"Little brother, you have been busy! Let's go out for some coffee tomorrow, just us two. Bring the copy and the diaries. You have got me *hooked* on this treasure story! Man, what if it could be true? Maybe a bucket of gold coins! Wouldn't that knock your socks off?"

X   X   X

Junior's coffee had been cold for over half an hour. Ed Had showed him several of the most interesting diary entries copied in the notebooks he'd bought. Ed was delighted at how fascinated his brother was as he read and read. The waitress sidled over, motioning toward the cup. Junior shook his head and kept on reading. He had come to Eli's entries about riding the paddle-wheeler on Lake Michigan.

12.9.25 Wind feerce aroun to the west mostly we not gittin south like we shuld. I heerd the Capt an Avery growsin each other las night

Avery sez hed south bufor the wether gits worsern now Capt sez were blowed way east an cant do nuthin bout it so Avery he reel mad the Capt sez hes the captin an wont lose his new ship over a pile a logs. They was that mad I tells you.

12.10.25 strong wind as yet but more northerly this day Capt. sez were goin to try south agin mebe git between hog and garden. Billy an mes shore perplexed bout whar we be goin now sounds like its on land somwhar where theys hogs got into the garden er somthin Billy sez. One a them saler boys lost a thum he was chippin ice offn the stays an the ax slipped an off she come slickern goose grees he hollered plenty but Captin jist laffed and sed the saler still gots one of them left anyways. Billyn me we dint laff that much musta been a hurt like youd niver bleeve it was his left hand so that's a good thang Im thinkin. Goin south now an them paddels shor werkin up the water theys somthin to see yessir they shorly air hows ennybody on a bote know whar in heck they air Billy sez. I agree with that not a tree ner a mounting no place to take a bearin on but Capt he looks threw this litel thang ever mornin when its sunny out an then he kin tell whar we air at I don't know how he does it but he does. Rites figgers down on one a them big charts an clames he knows mebbe he does fer a fakt I shor hope he does an no misteak on that thar. Wes a long way from Shicago I knows that shulda bin thar by now steem er sail but we aint.

12.11.25 A island comin up offn the starbort bow see how Im soundin like one a them sailer boys ha ha gittin mitey hi falutin that's me an Billy sez the same too. Capt sez it's a beaver but that don't make no sens to me but I aint no sailer even if I am talkin sailer talk an all. Averys in a *turribel mood an has bin fer days an days. Them padels actin up agin so who knows whatll happin. will we stop or is this a island with people or jist trees an rocks don't look like enybodys home on this hyar place but well see I rekon.*

"Want another donut?" Junior was putting on his coat. "We better be getting back, kid. They probably think we flew the coop. How are you and the old man getting along? He can be a bear, that's sure."

"Okay most of the time. I'm not very good at work in the shop, but I help him all I can."

"Let me give you a little 'big brotherly advice', Eddie. Get along with them even if it kills you! When you get older, especially if you get drafted, you'll think a lot differently about your parents. Take it from me kiddo, I've *been there!*"

"You've never said very much about what you did over there, Junior. Was it really bad? Course if you'd rather not talk about it that's o.k. I read your letters home, at least the ones Mom let me see."

"I don't mind telling you, but I still don't want Mom to hear some of what went on." They were at home in the driveway, still seated in Junior's Chevvy. "Isn't it about your chore time, Ed?"

"I got another hour or so. Dad milks two so I only have to milk old Curly. She kicked the bucket on me a while back. Lost most of the milk and put a big dent in the pail. Dad was really mad!"

Ed's brother didn't say anything for several minutes. He just sat, staring out of the windshield at nothing. "Hey Junior, I shouldn't have said anything about the war. Let's go in and get warm. I see Mom looking out the window. She's probably wondering what in the heck we're doing."

"Night dives were the worst." He spoke in almost a monotone, as if emotion was a thing to avoid. "I hated the night dives in training but that was nothing compared to combat. On Sicily, six of us had to go in before the troops were scheduled. Our big navy guns were lighting up the sky but we weren't worried about them. When we got close to the beach we started banging into stuff the enemy had installed. It was dark as pitch, probably about five a.m. or so. We set our charges and were waiting to get back to the ship when a round from the destroyer we were on fell short. I didn't know it then but my best buddy and two other Frogmen were blown to pieces by our own ordnance. The three of us who were still alive sure wanted to get out of there 'cause by then the Italian shore batteries were opening up on us. Trouble was the tide was coming in so fast we couldn't swim against it. It was starting to get light by then and small arms fire was churning up the waves. I got hold of one of the steel emplacements sticking up out of the surf and tried to hide behind it but it was only about six inches wide. You'd have laughed to see me trying to get that thin!

The guy who was assigned to me, 'my backwatcher' as I called him, was hiding behind some other junk four or five yards to my left. A bullet hit his facemask and tore it right off. The next shot killed him. I watched the whole thing. A bullet rattled the steel post I was hanging onto. It was time to get out of there! I detonated my three objectives, turned on my air valve and went under. The incoming tide was still pretty strong, but I made maybe a hundred yards back toward my ship. I thought I'd be o.k. then, so I jettisoned my tanks, surfaced and swam the rest of the way. The navy made me pay for the lost equipment!"

"Man oh man!" Ed whispered. Did you . . ."

"Enough, little brother. Let's go in. Remember, Mom don't need to know any of this."

Ed was very lucky that evening that old Curly didn't kick the bucket again! His mind was spiraling all over the place; upper Michigan logging, the treasure map, diaries, frogmen, everything but knowing when Curly had given all the milk she had to give!

Junior and family left Easter Sunday afternoon, as he had to be back at work on Wednesday. Beth cried and the baby cried too when they were finally packed in the Chevvy and pulling out of the driveway. Junior's wife, Jenny, had made a real hit with the family, even though the baby was "teething" and cried a lot. Ed felt awful. It seemed he was just starting to get to know his older brother when they had to leave. He promised to send Junior copies of the diaries every time he finished writing a few pages. It was plain that the ex-frogman was very interested in them and was taking the whole story seriously.

"Don't forget to put that kid's pencil copy of the map in with the first copied pages when you send them down to me. I can write in what those symbols and figures probably mean," Calvin Junior had told Ed when they were alone. Ed couldn't wait to finish the diary he was working on, so he could coax his mom to let him do the same with old Eli's first attempt. As far ss he knew it was still locked in the parlor cabinet.

12.13.25 I seen a lite on that island and tol the Captin he sed hed seen it too so I think weuns ankor an take the longboat in but Capt he sez no too much rocks an sech sez he. We sailed on south out from shor a ways them padel wheels not wirth dirt them clankin an bangin agin lucky the wind rite down from the north an west so makin good hedway under sails only. Come on a harber about sundown a cupla bildings peple waiving an shoutin for usun to come on in so we did that . Avery asts everbuddy he kin coller if theres a smithy they jist laffed it was lucky they were even a place to anker the boat. Capt wants to stay till the wind dyes sum but Avery crazy to git on down to Shicago like we was planning from the start. Winds rite Avery sez we kin go jist fine under sail all the way down the big lake to Shicago an sell our timber. up on the foredeck Billy sez why we have to go clar down to Shicago to sell timber plenny sawmills an sich way back from whar we come from first off I say the same too. Me an Billy wuld shor like to git a look at whats stored down in the hold Avery keeps close watch on the hatchway an when he don't them other 2 L.C. an J. W. does so no way to git down thar.

12.14.25 O Katy thangs heetin up I tells ya yessir. We slep last nite In a litel church an no fire but nice. bout 10 this a.m. there com a sloop an a purtier one you never seen. She was flhying a penant from Canady underneeth the ol Stars an Stripes. Well Avery yelling ever man on bord or be left behind he sez I an Billy jist walkin on the beech an had a ways to go to git on bord the Caroline. Captin was gittn up steem me an Billy we wunders how come since them padle wheels not goin good no way. Billy he runs fast an ketches the longboat but me I was goin back to that thar church to git my kit but Avery an the Capt not waitin fer no man ner beest. TheCaroline makin way outn the harber buffor I culd even git abord her Billy waving an yelling at me but it done no good atall she was on the way out. Them padels was makin a awful racket as theyd gone bad agin like I sed afor but the Caroline movin out smart as punch rite past that ere pertrol boat fer that's what that other boat was an no misteak. I heered a musket shot an yelling from the sloop but Capt an Avery not givinin a inch no siree they jist slipped rite past them others round the point they went tryun to git sails up too an did it. The sloop ups anker an tries to make there turn but wind agin em an no steem fer themuns no siree. Well sez I its stuck fer me an no misteak an me with hardlee no monee atall. Lucky I gots ol Betsy the long gun. Me an Billy bin doin a little huntin that morning gots my kit too sech as it is not much an that's fer shor but mebbe I kin hunt and fish fer the town folks till I gits offn this hyar island whenever that culd be don't know. Hope Billy an them is o.k. The pertrol boat finely got squared away an outn the harber but theres no way they gonna ketch Caroline even with them reel bad side padels. Steem gonna be the way a thangs from now on Im thinkin. I knowed all along them 3 Avery an LC an JW was up to sommthin or tother now looiks like the Captin in on it too. Hope Billy an them sailor boys not in trubbel over it caws they not have nothing to do with that other Just Billy loggin and them sailor boys jist ships men. I seen the chief a Chippeway Injun a good man so fars I kin see he sez

stay an hunt fer my keep. A boat comes from some place he calls charls
boys or somthin like that thar but never knows fer shor when the boat
comes. Jist wait an see I rekon.

"Got a letter from Junior today addressed to me. He's pretty
smart! There were actually two letters in it. One was for me to show
Mom and Dad, and the other one was secret. He's really getting into
the treasure hunt. That's what he calls it, 'our treasure hunt'."

Tom was impressed. "What did he say to you that your folks
weren't to know about?"

"Get this! He's got the copy of the map you made, and my copies
of the first fifteen pages of Eli's second journal. He's sure that the map
is real and . . .*he knows the place it's showing!*"

"Where, for Pete's sake?"

"You and me could tell it was a map of an island, but we didn't
know which one. I feel like such a fool because it's simple enough. It's a
rough map of Beaver Island in Lake Michigan!"

"How'd he figure it out?"

"It's so obvious. The diary says they were heading for Chicago. The
only way would be straight south on Lake Michigan, so Junior just got a
Michigan highway map and by comparing it with the journal entries it
was plain as day. Remember that double barred cross toward the
bottom of the map?"

"Of course I do! I drew up that whole thing, remember?"

"Well that's where he thinks the treasure is. Junior's pretty sure of it and I am too."

"But that cross wasn't on the island, it was off the edge a little ways. I remember it well."

"Sure! The treasure must be *under water!*"

12.18.25 Bad news this day fer shor a young'un playin down south beech a ways finds Billy that's rite Billy. He was neer ded but the kids mama tuk Billy in an they did as they culd fer him an sent fer me they knowed we was pals see. So I goes down thar fast as ever I culd hoof it. They'd put poor Billy to bed in there cabun an coverd him with 2 blankets theyd done all they culd them bein purty poor folks like neer all a them on that there island. Bad Luck Island I calls it an that's no misteak Billy reel bad hert and burnt all along a one side of im an bad hert in his back his legs cant hardly move neither one only a litel bit. What happen I ast him. Well ol Avery scairt of a pertrol boat after usns the wind not faverble no way so he sez more steem an Captin sez ya caint do her lest she blow up but you know ol Avery. He sez Billy you hold down that thar safety valv so I don that thar then what you thank the next thang he does wel he gits them sailer boys to cut the lashins on the timber an over the side they goes all a them big white pines weuns werked so hard fer all fall rite over the side they goes. Waves was high an bustin over the gunnels like as you never seen in your life. O I gess you did see that Billy sez to me thinkin bout that big blow weuns was in bufor. Then what happen I ast him. Billy he culd barly talk but doin his best it blowed up that's what the boiler split rite down the midel and steem everwhar. For I knowed it I was in the lake bad burnt an somthin bad gone all rong in my back he sez. One a them sailer boys he saved my bakin thats shor hoisted me up on some deck planks him bleedin bad his arm cleer gone one eer near tore off he saved me but not his own self he jist slid offn the planks an drownded. What about Avery an them I ast him them otherns he sed all dead an them too Billy kinda slep so me I slips out the door an let him sleep as he shor lookt bad an no misteak neither.

12.20.25 Billy near gone I thinkin caint eat nothing only wants water eyes bout haf open but he sees me an sez come on in he gots somthin to say to me he asts the womin an litel boy to go outside even if it is snowin like the dikens. They do go out an Billy canint hardly do moren whisper but he tries to an sez when the boiler blowed up they was a hole rite through the side of the Caroline. Avery an the Capt an 2 sailers was in the hold they was tryin to git at whatever was down thar but when the Caroline rolled over them hatches seezed up an they was trapt down in thar. Then she sank masts an all nothing but junk an sech spinnin round whar she went down. I seen alla this from them planks I was layin on. I heerd the Capt say that morning to Avery he sez if we go down recollect these hyar numbers. Them numbers tells rite whar the Caroline is layin on the bottom rite now so heres them numbers fer ye fer that's whar the Caroline is layin an whativers in them cases gots to be still thar. That's jist what my good frend Billy sed an heres them numbers. I gots a idee of what to do with em but not in this hyar diary yesir I got a reel good idee how to hide them numbers.

12.25.25 Billy cashed in his chips in the night. Wal its now Crismas Day an I jist thought heck fire I never give pore Billy no Crismas present. Some Crismas I say weuns was good frends an that's a fackt. Wal that thar very nite I gots busy tryin my hand at makin a map yessir a map never done sich of a thang bafor but no time like the presen Pa allus sed. Id walked purt neer all over that thar litel island huntin game Beaver is the proper name for her I sed that afor dint I so I had a fare to midlin idee of how that thar land layed. Dug out my old diary pensil and tried my luck. Reel lite at first. A bad job it twas and that's a fackt I showed the poor thang to that ol Injun mayor er cheef whatever he was he sed not too bad made a lotsa changes till he sed it was purty neer rite. I rote them numbers Billy told me about rite about on the place whar the water be about whar I figger the Caroline went down. Corse I dint tell nobiddy what I was up to no sirree I shor dint.

"You and your brother certainly are carrying on a lively correspondence! What's in all those letters anyway?"

Ed licked the stamp and pressed it down. "Junior wants to read the diaries, so I've been sending him my copies every time I get a few more done. And Mom, It's really hard trying to write the way your old great, great grandpa wrote. I guess you know that since you probably read them yourself."

"No Eddie, to tell the truth I really meant to finish reading them, but it seems like I've always been too busy. Just kept putting it off.

CHAPTER SEVEN

Treasure Plans

"Come on, turn the heater on. I'm *freezing!*"

"It don't work. And anyway I can't afford to waste the gas. You're always cold, Tom. What's wrong with you anyway?"

"You say you got another secret letter from your brother in Louisiana? What's the scoop? Is he still going to help us find a million in gold?"

"What do you mean *us?* When I find the treasure, and by golly I'm going to, it'll be mine! *All mine!*"

"Then why am I freezing to death in this old egg beater you call a car? I want my share, same as you."

They were silent for a while. Ed allowed the suspense to build, in order to let his friend   wonder what the final deal was going to be. Tom could be a pretty stubborn guy, and Ed was well aware of it. He thought he'd better end the game before Tom got really mad. Still he said nothing, enjoying the way he was keeping his buddy in the dark. Finally he grinned and said, "O.k., O.k., just kidding. You help me get the treasure and, well since you and I have been such good pals, some of it will be yours, I promise."

"How can I help? You've got the map. Or your brother does. What's the latest installment on the 'chronicles of Eli'? Does Junior know I'm in on the whole thing? And does he know who made that beautiful copy of the original?"

"He knows all about you Tom. Don't get mad. Listen it's going to take two of us to make a go of this venture. So you're definitely in. That is if you want to be."

"Man you're serious aren't you? Do you really have a plan or are you just blowing off steam? I want the story. All of it!"

"Right. Here's what's happened. Junior was a navy Frogman. Did you know that?"

"Sure I knew. Everybody at school heard about how he and some buddies would swim underwater to the beaches before the troops came in. Blew up mines and stuff, didn't they?"

"They sure did. The thing is though, he had all this training to read maps, use underwater air tanks, all that stuff. So . . . in his latest letter [secret from Mom and Dad] he *knows* where the treasure is! See, those numbers and stuff you copied were what he calls coordinates. He took your drawing, enlarged it and laid it over a real Coast Guard chart of the water all around Beaver Island. He can tell us just how far off shore it is and everything!"

"Where what is?"

"The spot where the ship went down when the boiler blew up."

"I am lost! What are you *talking* about?"

"Shoot! I forgot that you haven't had a chance to read the last few diary entries. I'll bring them to school tomorrow, but you better not let *anybody* see them! I mean not anybody! If this gets around it could mess up the whole deal."

"Oh, all right. I'll keep them out of sight, but I've got a question for you. If your brother is so excited about the treasure and knows right where it's supposed to be, what's to stop *him* from bringing it up himself? He's got all that underwater gear he uses for the petroleum company he works for. Maybe he's just pulling your leg. Like it's a great big joke on little brother."

"I thought of that too, Tom. In fact I have to admit you're 'playing second fiddle' on this caper. I asked Junior if he and I could go up there this summer and stay till we found the goodies."

"Thought so. What did he say?"

"What would you expect? He's *married* for crying out loud! They want to buy a house, so he's working all the overtime he can get. Summer's the busiest season, since the water is a little warmer and there's less storms. He can't go, and that's it."

"You really talking about going? Going this coming summer?"

"I am Tom, and I was hoping you'd go too. What do you say?"

"*Come on* Ed! I'm broke and I strongly suspect that you're

broker than me. What would we use for money?"

"Junior suggested a plan which sounds like it could work. When he was about sixteen, like we are, he worked picking cherries in the orchards around Traverse City, Michigan. They pay according to how much you pick. They pay everybody off at the end of each day , so you can quit any time. I looked in the atlas at school and Traverse City is not far from the town of Charlevoix where you get the ferry to Beaver Island. What do you think?"

"I think you and your brother are both nuts, but I'll sure think about it. Would this be in July or August?"

"No way. The cherries get ripe in June. Another thing. If you do decide to go with me we don't tell anybody, especially our parents, about trying to find the treasure. It's just a couple weeks in the summer to make some money. That's what I'll tell my folks and you better do that too. That is *if* you really decide to do this."

Tom was silent for quite a while. "I'd better be getting home. I'll think about it, O.K.?"

"You do that, and watch your mouth, you hear?"

X   X   X

Tom struggled to make sense of Eli's spelling and lack of almost any punctuation. It took all of his one study hall to figure it out. "Why'd Ed have to write this the way the old geezer wrote it?" he thought,

Excitement was building nevertheless. He couldn't help grinning a little as he headed off to math class. "What if this whole thing is really true?" he kept thinking. "It must be true though. Ed's mom has had the diaries for a long time, and they were given to her after somebody old in her family died. There's no way she would fake something like this! And it looks like Ed's folks didn't know anything about the map he dug out of that old gun barrel. I think it must be the real thing. *A real treasure!* Can't believe it! I'll bet it was silver in those cases. Nobody could get that much gold back then. Don't they mine silver in Canada someplace? Bet that's it all right. I'll see if Ed has an idea of what the treasure is. Or maybe his brother has said something about what it is down there on the bottom of Lake Michigan." His mind was spinning!

12.29.25 It shor is lonely without my good fren Billy he war shor one gud un thats sartin me an him was clsot even if we hadn knowed each other but a few months. Whats to do now is what Im thinkin gotto git pore Billy in the groun but it froze hard the groun is so that thar ol Injin hes some kinda mayor er something sez theys a litel sematery back of the church an I kin bild a far to thaw the groun till weuns kin dig up a grave fer my ol pal Billy. We done this an it was hard goin til we gots bulow the frost line an no misteak about that fer shor. An ol woomin sed some reel nice prayin an bout everbuddy on that thar island come to the funreal I dint even know por Billys last name nor whar he come from nor whar his wife and babee were at dint make no diffrens anyways I thinks as he don have nuthin to send em nohow. A sad day an no misteak but we done all weuns culd fer the por cuss. But whats to become a me now no monee Mam an Pap gots no idee whar I am at or whats to come next. The ol Injun mayer sez thars a boat comes some times they never knows when fer shor but he sez soon fer the harber be froze bufor long aint that too bad but Im hopin she gits here soon sos I kin git offin this hyar island. If I does then I rites to the Compny Avery werkt fer an tell themuns what all went on. Mebbe they send me a letter with my loggin wages I shorly hopes so least ways. Mebbe they kin tell me whar Billys wife an chile is. If they kin I'll send what I kin to em an no misteak about that Billy so proud a his missus an litel babee a sad thing alla this bin. Avery an them other 2 an the Capt too was in on some bad bidness or tother sartin shor but thems under the waves now fer shor.

12.30.25 No boat come yet everbuddy on this hyar island waitin fer it ever day I think they gits mail an grub an sich so theys mitey ready fer that boat that's sartin.

1.1.26 A new year. Shor hope its bettern the last one no boat but some more huntin tuday twarnt easy that's shor. Fust off I had used up all my shot an lead to make bullets but they was a kid some sorta cuzzzin of that thar Injun mayer had bout 6 er 7 bullets all made up told him Id give him some of the meat ifn I kilt somthin fer them bullets. They was the wrong size too big by a mite but Im not a gent to let thangs git me down so I went rite to werk on them 6 er 7 he gimme borried a file an went to werk on em to git em round as they needs to be. Finelyt thot 1 of em was neer enuf so went huntin that leetle crooked slug rammed down hard in the barrel had to borry a litel powder too as I hadn none a that thar left neether. A purty pore hunter was I an no misteak.

Bout sundown it gittin neer too dark to see this litel spiked buck deer comes a shashayin outn the bresh not moren 2 rods from me hidin behind some bushes put the beed on him rite back a the sholder like Pap allus tole me wal that ball a lead wasn neer rond enuf so warnt true atall aimed rite at the the sholder like I sed an cut loose hit that yearling buck rite in the neck kin you bleeve that haha. Paps old gun Betsy never shot strate atter that even if I did try her twicet mor. Finely one a them not round bullets got stuck hard down by the breech an do you think I culd budge her out no siree. Knowin me I has a idee rite off. I tuk that thar map of the island Beaver Island is what its called proper roled up the map tite as a tick an jist pushed her down till it struck the lead ball already stuck in thar. Then I takes another ball an did likewise so now the map all seeled up fer good an all. You thank that wasn smart wal you gots a nother think comin

1.2.26 she come tuday an ever buddy clamerin an happy as clams. Me too as now I gots a chanct to go to the maneland next day finely. Them island fokes bin reel gud to me an no misteak. Id shor pay em back but they sez no to that yessir theys fine fokes fer shor. I left em the deer meat.

X   X   X

"Dad, you got a minute?" Ed had finished his homework, Beth was sewing on a pair of socks, his dad falling asleep behind his newspaper. The paper rattled and Cal's eyes popped open.

"What did you say?"

"I wanted to talk to you and Mom about something."

"Go ahead," Beth said putting her sewing aside. "We're listening. Are you in some kind of trouble?"

"You better *not* be" Cal growled, fixing his eyes on his son.

"No! No, I'm not in any trouble at all. It's about this summer."

"What about it?"

"Dad, I've been wondering if I could get a part-time job this summer. My car needs a new radiator and a couple tires. You said keeping it up was my responsibility so I'll need to make some money."

"Planning to leave me with all the farm work are you? You know how much there is to do during the summer. I don't like the sound of this at all."

"What kind of job are you thinking about, Eddie? I doubt if the Stubers will need extra help this summer, since their son is home from the army," his mother said, trying to ease the tension.

"No, Dad, I know how much there is to do. I'm really only thinking about three weeks or so. Just in June. I'd be back in time for the second hay cutting and getting the wheat off."

"Back from *where?*" his dad demanded.

It was time to play his 'ace in the hole'. "Well," he began, "Junior told me how he worked in the cherry orchards in Michigan a couple summers. They start in early June, and usually are all finished in about three weeks. I don't remember him doing that, but I guess I was too young then."

Cal actually smiled a little. "That *Junior!*" he sighed. "He was a go-getter that's sure. So he told you about that did he? That brother of yours was a worker, I'll tell you. I always figured he'd be a mechanic some day. He was a wonder with tools."

"What do you think, Dad? Mom?"

"Cal Junior's got good sense. If he thinks you can do it and make some money, then it's o.k. with me. What do you say, Mother?"

"How far is it? Where would you stay? If you'd need to pay room and board you surely wouldn't be able to save much money," she said.

"Junior stayed in our old umbrella tent. Did his own cooking and everything. Sometimes he said the farms would let him camp right in the orchard. It didn't cost him a dime for any lodging."

"That kid was sure something! Still is!" Cal said.

"But wouldn't you be all alone there? Camping and everything?"

"Gee, Mom, if Junior did it I can too. I'll have my car, and maybe I could use the two-burner kerosene stove you use for canning in the cellar. I'd write to you sometimes so you'd know I was o.k., and it won't be that long anyway. Junior says the whole picking season only lasts about three weeks, or at least it did when he was there."

Nobody said anything for a few minutes. When Ed couldn't stand the suspense any longer he held his breath, then blurted out *the question.* "Well, can I go or not?"

"You can go, but I want one week of help with the first hay cutting. That should be around June first, depending on the weather. Then you are to be back and ready to work by July first. It might be sooner too, if the wheat ripens early."

Ed could hardly keep from, yelling "yippee!" or something, but he held it in. His dad headed out the door. Beth began to clear the table, but watched out the window until she saw the lights come on in the shop. "You just sit right there for a minute, Eddie. You and I need to talk about this."

"But Mom," Ed began, "Dad said it was o.k. You're not going to keep me from going are you?"

"Well we'll see. But first I want some things cleared up."

"What things?"

"You've been seeing a lot of Tom Dillon lately. I'm not blind or stupid. Are you planning to ask him to go with you?"

"Well Mom you see . . . uh . . that is . . ."

"The truth son! But you've already told me that. If your Father knew you were going to ask Tom, he would *never* have said yes."

"For Pete's sake Mom! How long is he going to hold a grudge against me? And Tom too? We're not going to do anything that crazy ever again! You won't tell him will you?"

"I won't tell him, but if he finds out and forbids you to go, I'll do the same."

"Thanks Mom! Could you give me some cooking lessons before we . . I mean *I go?* I can do eggs and fried potatoes and bologna, but not much else."

She laughed, rumpled his hair and started the dinner dishes.

X   X   X

1.3.26 Thangs shor hoppin an no misteak. I gots hyar to Charlys Boy aint that a funny name fer a town? No monnee nor knowed no buddy hyar in this town and the supply boat wanting payed fer my passage purty bad they took me to the plice stashion an that thar were the best thang fer me. It turned out them cops had heered bout Billy dead and the Caroline sunk they wanted me to make a statement as they called it so I done that. Youd be sprized what next happens they sent a tell a gram to the loggin Co. theys to send a man down hyar to see about these doins with Billy the Caroline Avery an the timber. The whole durn shootin match may be they pay me my wages and git werd to Billys fambly if they knows whar they is at. Im sleepin in the jail but them cops bin nice the foods purty good an no werk to do nor nothing so thangs culd be a lots worse an no misteak on that thar. 1.4.26 Nothin happen taday yit. 1.5.26 turribel snow alla last nite an taday so still no men from the logginCo.1.6.26 They come taday an what a story theys tellin. After ol Avery an us left on the Caroline he never payed them others of our loggin crew. The men from the Co. sed we shulda bin payed ever 2 weeks but that not what Avery told us. He sed wed git our pay at the jobs end er some such but then I mighta knowed hed lye but then he did save Billy when he went over the rale so it peers he warnt all bad an anyways its bad luck to talk bad about dead fokes so I dint. I never told them Co. men about them cases hid down in the hold of the ol Caroline but the poleece was askin a lotsa questions so I knowed them from that thar purtrol boat tol em some thang that's fer shor but I sed not a thang no siree I dint caws I aim to git whats in that sunk ship if there be a way to do it but I shor don't know how it culd be done an no misteak. 1.7.26 Nothin happen taday not yit any how. Cops was after me agin but theys purty shor I not in on what they was worryin about with them cases an all. I kep still lessen they ast me somthin which they done a lotta times an even when theys done I kep my head an give em nothing to rite up in them litel books they had with em. Acours I dint say nothin bout these books a mine I bin ritin in kep em hid in the bottom of my lunch pale thar bein nothing in it but a peese a bread I keeps in thar on top a muy papers to fool em and it does too.

X   X   X

Tom traded Ed half a sandwich for two cookies. They gulped milk from the little boxes and continued digging into their brown paper lunch bags. "I'm getting so I can read those diary entries about as fast as if they were regular English." Tom said, slurping a swallow of milk. "If you just sort of read fast and don't mind the fact that there just aren't hardly any periods or commas it's really easy."

"You should try copying those pages just like old Eli wrote them! I tell you it's almost impossible. Then when I get going on the copies, I find myself doing my homework like that!"

"Why do you do it?"

"I promised Mom I'd take care of the original entries, and I'm going to, as best I can anyway. I told you there's another book just like this one didn't I?"

"Yeah, you told me. Hey, maybe that other book would tell us what the treasure is or something more we could use. Do you think?"

"No, I don't think so. The one we're working on is the second one, so it's later than the other. I think Mom will let me copy that first one later, as long as I don't mess up with this one."

"Heard anything more from you brother?" Tom asked, Wadding up his empty lunch bag.

"Not for a while. I keep sending him my copies as soon as I get four or five pages done. He's really busy, and I don't suppose there's much more he can tell me. I wish he would come home again. I'd sure like to talk to him about all of this."

"Maybe we could talk to him about coming up to Michigan and helping us find the treasure this summer," Tom said, as they headed back to class.

"Mom and Dad got another letter yesterday. He didn't

say anything to me in it, but he told them that he and his wife and kid might, he said *might* , be sent over to Lebanon this spring. The company he works for is trying to get some sort of oil deal over there. He says if it works out, in one summer he can make enough money to get a down payment on a house!"

"Where in the heck is *Lebanon?*"

"I looked it up. It's close to the Holy Land and on the Mediterranean Sea. I suppose he'd be diving there some place. I'm not sure. Mom's really worried. She doesn't want them to go, but Dad says, 'Make the bucks while you can.' Maybe he won't go and could get a vacation or something this summer. Of course his wife will have something to say about all of that!"

"Hey Ed, I asked my folks and they said I could go cherry picking with you this June. How about that, huh?"

"Great! But remember, don't let my dad know you're going with me. He's still mad about the cider barrel."

"Well gee whiz, *you* were in on it too! What right's he got to blame me any more than his own kid?"

"Hold on Tom. It's not that he blames you any more than me, but he thinks us two guys going up there together will probably rob a bank or something. So just keep it quiet, o.k.?"

"How we going to do that, though?" Tom asked as they piled into their seats for geometry class.

"I've got it figured, I think. But we better cool it now. Schaffer's giving us the eye."

CHAPTER EIGHT

Billy's woman

1.8.26 Gittin mitey tired a sleepin in the jailhouse but the Co. men come taday an gess what. They took me to a nice restrant an dint do a thang but bot me a reel nice meal yessiree thay shor done that I thinks they skeered a me that may be I caws them some truble er other over not gittin payed off like I shulda an Billy too. Corse hes ded now so no matter to him an no misteak on that. I bout fell over when them Co. men talked so nice an not only that thar but payed me off ever penny I had comin they shorly did. They had them greenbacks to pay me with but Im no fuel. Silver sez I that be what I want so one of em run to a little bank clost by an shor enuf come back with a tote bag of them big silver dollars you culd hardlee bleeve it so meny of em a hunert an 9 what s you thank a that. Them Co. men asts some of the same thangs them cops did but not too much. A reel gud thang. Them Co. men sed theyd git me home or wharever an no cost to me neether another good thang they knows whar at is Billys woman an litel un that thar a reel good thang an no misteak on that me I gots some heavy thinkin to do for shor. Billys woman livinup thar at Mackingnaw town I was thar onct on the way up to the loggin camp not much thar but the army fort. I slep in the guardhouse one night thar at that army fort they was reel snotty at me but I dint care let em sez I long as they lets me sleep inside outn the rain an skeeters like they done. This hyar Mackingnaw town not that thar Mackingnaw island whar we stopped off a cupla days on are way to the loggin camp. That island shoir was jumpin trapers injuns solders fancy men an women too I spect. Furs everwhar stacked up in big barns like a things monee bein throwed ever which way but none throwed to me haha. I war that reddy to git offn that thar divils playgroun an thats a fackt. Seen no sine of the late war up thar on that island it bein over fer 6 er 8 yars. Don't nobuddy seem to keer about it no more one way or tother Frechies Englishmens Irish Sweeds an who knows what else on that litel island glad to git ofn her without loosin Paps monee nor my long gun an no misteak. Then weuns on the way to the big woods to git started in the loggin. Billys woman werkin in a litel bakery thar at Mackingnaw town not that thar island jist on land that about all them Co. men knows but her name Roseen they tol me how to spell it she sorta a Frenchie I rekon most of em are up thataway anyhow. Wal thars some thangs I gots to do so I jist done it. Bought a bag a flour cornmeal sugar an a side a bakin the mail boat to see that they be taken to the Beaver island whar I jist got off of. Don't hardly trust no buddy whar silver consarned so I hid 5 of them shiney dollars in each sack. The Capt. Likes me now sins I payed my fare so he sez he see that the goods gets to the old Mayer to pass around. O an another thang I sent a big poke a hard candee fer the younguns over on that Beaver island I felt good that I done this as they treeted me an Billy reel good even if they hadn hardly nothing thereselves neether. Don't trust no buddy whar silver monee consrned that's why I hid them silver dollars inside a them pokes of vittels thataway I knows they gits to the iujun mayer at leest. Still thinkin whar I goes sins them Co. men sez I kin go jist about any wheres they shor bin nice I almost wunders why they is so nice but don't look a gift horse in the mouth my ol Pap allus sez so I don't. A idee buzzin around in my old head an more an more I thinks I gots a nother job to do bafor I gits home to Ohiya an Mam an Pap.

X   X   X

Junior's letter made Beth anxious and a little upset. He and his wife and daughter were going to Lebanon for sure. They were very busy making final arrangements, so would not be able to make a trip to Ohio or West Virginia where Jenny came from. They were planning to hang onto their apartment while they were over there, since housing was very scarce in 1946. The servicemen and women were coming home and they all needed a place to live. Junior and Jenny had had no trouble finding a young couple to live in their apartment until they came back from Lebanon. Junior figured they would be over there for at least a year.

Ed was a model workman on the farm, not wanting to further anger his dad. He lugged the old umbrella tent up from the cellar and took it to the barn. He pulled the hay wagon out of the big double doors to make room for the tent. He wished Tom could be there to help, but that was out of the question. His dad eyed the tent but said little about it at first. Finally he walked up and watched his son struggling with the heavy canvas. "Junior would have had that thing up and ready an hour ago," he said, hands on hips. "You better learn to handle that tent if you think you're going to be living in it for a month.

The way you got it there the first wind that came along would have the whole thing down around your ears!"

Ed bit his tongue to keep from lashing out at the man. "He might give me a hand," he thought bitterly. "So I'm *not* Calvin Junior. So *what?* I'll get this thing up when we get to Michigan. I'm just practicing now. Man, will I be glad to get away from here!" It was only the end of April so he would have a while to wait.

Junior's final letter included a page for Ed. In it he suggested that if his younger brother was really planning to work in the orchards, he should write to the Traverse City Chamber of Commerce for instructions and suggestions. It was an excellent idea, and would save a great deal of time for anyone planning to work during the coming season. Ed did so and a reply came in a short time. He put all the papers in the bottom of his mom's old suitcase so he wouldn't forget them.

The Ford needed some work, so after chores every Saturday he tried to get the old beater in shape. He put "stop-leak" in the radiator, along with a bottle water glass which would temporarily seal the fine crack in the motor block. His trapping money was about gone, but his mom sneaked him a few dollars from her "butter and egg money".

"That car still using oil?" Ed jumped at his father's totally unexpected remark.

"Yeah, but not too much Dad."

"Well there's a case of W-30 under the bench in the tractor shed. You better pack it in your car somewhere. Be sure to check your oil every time you stop on the way. Give the old buggy a drink if she needs it. It'll get you there. Junior took mighty good care of that car."

"Gee, thanks Dad. I didn't know what I was going to do about oil. I'll keep checking. It probably needs some right now."

"That case is for the trip. Don't get into it before then!"

Beth secretly poked her son in the ribs, a little smile curling around her lips. It was a nice gesture, and one that was not easy for her husband to make. Ed went upstairs to do some more "translating" as he thought of it.

X   X   X

1.9.26 My minds made up an no misteak about that them Co. men wantin to git goin so I sez boys I wants to go up to Mackingnaw town not to home like I sed bafor. They was shor happy fer that war the very place they come from. There big offus was up thar an so we could all go an save the Co. some monee too. I was shor I had to see Billys woman an young'un them Co. men sez they never give her no monee yit as thy dint know whar Billy was an the wages was hisn to do with. Them not knowin nothin about pore Billy bein dead and berried on that island so they sed first thang we comes to Mackingnaw town theyd find her an setel up with her what was to bin Billys. We gots on a stage to a town I fergit its name then on a purty good road north don't know why Im still

*scribblin on hese hyar pages but I got kinda used to doin it. Don't hurt nothing nor cost nothing so why not sez I. Course I still don't let them Co. men know about this ritin Im doin jist bein keerful is all. 1.10.26 Staid in a reel nice tavern last nite themCo. men got a litel lowd with som wiskey but not me I savin my dollars sins it any buddys gess when I git some more . Curios to see Billys woman I know shes purty sins Billy was allus showin that litel tintype of her. Sad thang he ast fer it when he all burnt an busted up. Them peepel helped him nice when he was in there cabin but that thar picture gone to the bottom with the Catroline I spect. So I tells him Id git it tomorrow an that made him feel a litel better. Then he up an died that nite so he never knowed the pcture was gone an that war a good thang Im thinkin. 1.11.26 No ritin atall taday too bouncy on the stage so mebbe tamarrow well see then.
1.12.26Finely got hyar it bein almost dark wes purty tired them Co. men don't like ridin much cant blame em cold an bumpy an slow goin. Gots up to the attick whar she stayin Billys woman that is an the little un too a course. I tol her all about Billy but never sed nothing bout how burnt and broke up in his back an legs neether. She cryed some wal whats you expect she bin missin him her Billy I meen fer a long time so she cryed whilst I set on the bed theres no chares in the litel room to set on. That young'un reel pert litel thang she cryed some too caws her momma was an she not knowin why I spect. Had a litel trundel bed under neeth the big bed an that's whar she Renays her name slept at. The moms name is Roseen purty name I sez I to meself. I slep that nite in a roomin house me bein rich an all HaHa. 1.13.26 Snowed youd not bleev las nite an taday too theys a litel genrel store rite clost by here so I bot her a dress*

may not ber the rite size ner nothing an fer the litel un a sorta dress
thang the stor lady sed would be good fer the chile. Tuk em up thar to
that attick but theys gone She workin in a litel bakery in that thar
Mackingnaw town whar we is at. She keeps the baby rite in the back
room of the bakery. I went to see em she was busy but I tol her Id take
em both out to eat at the roomin house Im at. That nite. couldnt hardly
wait but went to the Co. place an they sed theyd give her Billys wages
this same nite as were to eat our supper at the roomin house whar at
Im stayin shined my ol shoes er tried to anyways. Thar bein no axel
grees I could find I asts the roomin house lady to gimme a spuneful a
bakin drippins she done that an dint charge nuthin neether even gimme
a pees a muslin jist a litel pees but enuf im thimnkin. I soked that thar
muslin reel good with the drippins an jist rubed an rubed on my ol boots
youd be sprized at how them ol clodhoppers shined up an no misteak. It
was dum misteak tho I went out to the litel genrel stor an I thinks ever
stray dog in Mackingnaw town follerin after me how dum kin one man
be the more them curs liked em the shinyer my ol boots got ha ha.

Got the roomin house ladys darter to shave me an cut my hair felt purty
tony then an no misteak on that thar. She Roseen wearin the dress I lef
at her atick it a mite too big but bettern what she had bafor the chile
Renay was wearin her new duds an so prowd youd jist laff to see it I dint
laff tho that mite a made em feel bad. The Co. men was in a awful hurry
it looked like but they brung her Billys wages like they sed they would I
never ast her how much monee it was but rekon about the same as me.
She Roseen jist about falls over seein all them bills in a litel sak from the
Co. Id git silver I tol her but she never did has her own ways Im findin

out she shor purty but kinda skiny like. The baby Renay looks helthy Id say. Youd be sprized if I tol you that leetel Renay she took to me rite away Im sprized my own self glad tho. I gots a bee a buzzin round in my ol hed agin an misteak about that thar neether.

X   X   X

When Ed got home from school he found his mom sitting at the kitchen table. She had a letter in one hand and a tissue in the other.

"What's wrong, Mom?"

"We got a letter from Junior and Jenny today. He mailed it from New York City. They're on their way by now. Out on the Atlantic. All three of them even the . . . the baby . . . out on that big ocean! Oh how I wish they'd stayed in the States. It was bad enough when they were all the way down there in Louisiana. *Now this!*" She cried a little but finally got up and handed him the letter. "You read it," she said, sniffing and rubbing her eyes. "You got much homework? Oh I forgot, it's Friday. You better get changed and at your chores. Dad wants to get done early so we can go over to the Lathams' place. They've got a new colt and your dad won't rest until he gets to see it. Do you want to come along?"

"Gee Mom, I don't think so. Do you mind if I don't go?"

"No I guess not. Do you mind getting yourself something to eat after chores? We're invited over there for supper. Are you sure you don't want to come along? May's a wonderful cook. Probably have blueberry pie. Your favorite!"

"No I don't really want to go. Do you think Dad will be mad?"

"I don't think so, but why don't you offer to milk one of his cows? That way we can get an earlier start, and that ought to put him in a good mood."

"Mom, you're a real *winner!* I'm gonna change and get at it."

The truck pulled out while he was still milking the second cow. He kept his mind on his business and both knees clamped on the bucket. Milking done, he even took a half hour to clean two stalls. He was taking no chances! He could almost feel the silver from the treasure dribbling through his fingers. Back in the house, he was making himself a fried egg sandwich and re-reading junior's letter. It was then that it hit him! He dropped the sandwich and read the letter again. There was a P. S. at the bottom. He'd read the whole letter before, including the post script but hadn't realized what it might mean.

P.S. tell Eddie to check at the post office once in a while. I

can't be sure if my letters will get clear out to the farm. A

letter might just make it that far. – Cal Jr.

The sandwich forgotten, he was on the phone to Tom in less than a minute. He read the post script and waited for his friend's reaction.

"I don't see what's so important about that. Sounds to me like your brother just wants to be sure you guys get all the stuff he sends. Probably don't know how the mail will come through from way over there in . . . where is it he's going?"

"Man, you are *dense!* Don't you see? He said for *me* to check at the post office. Don't that seem kind of funny? Why not just say to check it? Anybody going into town could do it, but he said *me!*"

"I still don't get it. What are you talking about?"

"I think he's going to write to me, but just address it to me at 'general delivery.' If he's got stuff for me that he don't think Mom and Dad should know about, I'll get it that way, and they won't know."

"You think so?"

"I'm sure of it! Man, I'll be checking in at the old post office any day I drive to school."

"But with no basketball practice anymore your dad will probably say no to you driving to school instead of taking the school bus. I've heard how he hates to waste gas."

"Wait a minute. You're right. Say . . when does baseball practice start? Pretty soon, right?"

"It's started already, but just for pitchers and catchers in the gym till the weather breaks. Then it'll be outside. Why? You're no baseball player."

"Tommy my friend, I just got an awful craving to become a catcher on our baseball team! Guess then I'll have to drive to school.

So I can stay for baseball practice. Won't that be awful?"

"Not a bad idea but I see a slight problem."

"You think so? What problem?"

"I've played pitch and catch with you since we were kids. You can't catch a *cold,* let alone a baseball!"

"Heck, I know that. I'll either be cut from the squad or I'll have to quit, but Mom and Dad don't have to know whether I'm still practicing or not. I'll check the general delivery window at the post office a couple times a week. I'll bet you two bucks I get a letter from Junior as soon as they get settled over there in Lebanon. Just you wait!"

X   x   x

1.14.26 Roseen quit her job taday sed she had nuff monee fer a wile I glad she done that thar. I got em a room rite next to mine jist down the hall a litel ways we bin eetin reel good the roomin house lady a good cooker but she shor keepin a eye on thangs tho feered me an Roseen mite git too close I reckon. That be jist fine with me caws I don't want no buddy tellin tales outn school. That bee shor buzzin moren mort tho in my ol head I never scared a nothing much my hole life like bears mean horses tuff fellers an such but my ol knees jist a nockin ever time I thinks about what I bin thinkin about an no misteak. I finely ast her at supper wuld she want to go with me down Ohiya way to Mam an Paps farm we gots a litel cabin buhind the house she and Renay be reel snug in thar an me farmin an she mebbe help Mam er some such. You thinkin bout usns marryin up Roseen sez surprised like. why no I weren't neether sez I. I jist thot it mite be somthin. I spil tmy soup all over my new stor bot shert an litel Renay laff an then weuns all laffin. Wal she sez then I goes no place atall with you ner no buddy else lessen I gots a ring on my finger. I neer spilt ever thang wen she sed that thar then I sez you want to an she sez she does wanta so gess what weuns goin to the litel church rite here in Mackingnaw town an git hitched I caint hadlee bleeve it. She gimme a kiss on my cheek jist bafor her an the litel un went on down to there room I like to died rite thar an no misteak. Aint like I never bin kist bafor one time in school I had to rite somthin on the blckbord an the teacher Miz Polly sez Eli you don't have no grammer atall Wal sez I gess I do too my grammer 89 yars old names Gertrood an lives over this side a Molster. Wal all thekids a laffin they heds off an Miz Polly dint do a thang but made me set on the naughty stool back by the cote rack me bein bout 6 foot tall an oldern the teacher an all. Wal wen all them otherns gone out a thar she dint do a thang but pulld my ol hed down an kist me rite on my cheek. I had a 2 mile walk to home but I sware my ol feets never teched ground all that thar way ha ha Miz Polly not no ways neer to Roseen tho. Mam if yer readin this hyar wal that be the way it is an no misteak. 1.15.26 Gittin reddy taday my ol hed spinin caint think a nothing but them 2 an me.1.16.26 Roseen gots a mind a her own I tells ya she sez no buddy goin to no church drest like no tramps er bums neether so we gots a carrage to a bigger town I fergit its name an I neer coulda died she spent monee so fast but I so happee I dint care none we both gots monee any ways so that be the way. You shulda seen them 2 in them clothes she bot. Purtyern a new borned calf.

She gots me a cote an a reel gennelmans hat can ya bleeve that weuns to be at the church house 7 oclock so we et in a restrant in that thar town jist like rich folks an no misteak. She kep on lookin at me an I knowed I was sposed to do some thang but I dint know what it was we got in the carrage to git usuns back to Mackingnaw town an she look kinda sad like purty in them new close tho kep lookin at her hand till dum me finely got the pitcher she sed bafor bout a finger ring an I plum fergot. But youuns knows me from all this ritin I bin doin bafor. I gots a plan fer shor. Bafor we goes to the church house I slip away an find the roomin house woomans darter the one as had shaved me an tole her what a durned fuel I was she sed she knowed jist what needed done. She gits a litel box it all fancy an all with some doodads an sech in it she pict out a ring from thar twasnt very big but that jist what be fine fer Roseens litel fingers Im thinkin. Wal ths gal no fuel not like I am anyways she sez 3 dollars knowed I hadn no choice in the matter I knowed that litel ring not werth no 3 dollars 6 bits more like it but no time to haggle tho. Pap woulda skun me alive fer gittin tuk like that but I had my mind on other thangs. I payed her an put the litel ring in my poket then fer onst I done the rite thang. Id seed a litel tiny hart like of a thang on a litel chane in that thar box a hers how much sez I. 4 dollers she speeks rite up she lernin fast that un is. That thar thang likely tern green after a week er 2 warnt werth neer no 4 dollars 4 bits mebbe but then I jist in a awful herry may be I in luv er somthin my o my. A corse I payed her that too an put it in my other poket then I is reddy to git hitched up an no misteak about that thar atall.

X   X   X

Ed lasted four days until the coach came over to him, put an arm around his shoulders and whispered, "Ed, you're not a bad basketball player. If you keep working on fundamentals I could probably get you in some varsity games next year. At least you'd get lots of playing time on the reserve team. Maybe enough to earn a letter. That's *basketball!* You just don't have it in baseball. Surely you know that by now."

"I know coach," Eddie replied. "I've been thinking about quitting the team. Do you think that would be best?"

"It sure would," he answered, obviously much relieved that it went so easily. "You'd do better concentrating on basketball. No hard feelings?"

"No, Coach, no hard feelings at all!"

Eddie walked out of the gym, conscious of the stares of the other team members. He grinned a little, which caused some surprised looks. His plan hadn't worked out anyway. He'd checked at the post office regularly, but nothing came. His folks had received an airmail letter with no problem, so it looked as if he'd jumped to the wrong conclusion. Tom had a laugh about that, and Ed quit checking.

A couple days later Tom jumped off his school bus and came running up as Ed was walking into school. "Listen man," he whispered, "guess what? We were in town yesterday and just for fun I slipped into the post office. You know what I did? I told them I was *you,* and asked if there was any mail. She said there *was!* I asked her for it but she said she needed to see my driver's license. Well I just told her I didn't have it with me and got out of there. But it's *there* and your name's on it! Did you drive to school today?"

"I sure did! My folks don't know I got kicked off the baseball team. I'm heading for town the minute school's out. Man Oh *man!* I was right. Junior's got something to tell me about the treasure or something. I just know it! Want to come along? I could take you home after that."

"Darn it, I can't," Tom groaned. "I'm on that dumb committee for decorating the gym, and we're supposed to meet right after school."

"You're going to decorate for the prom already? That's kind of early aint it?"

"Naw, we're just getting ideas and stuff. The girls will make all the decisions but Jamison says there should be boys on the committee too. I don't know what for. Listen, call me tonight and tell me what's in that letter."

"I can't. They'd hear me. I'll see you in third period study hall tomorrow."

CHAPTER NINE

Spring, 1946

Ed sat in his car and opened the letter, eager to see what his older brother had to say to him.

"Hi kid' hope you got this letter o.k. I probably shouldn't be doing this stuff behind Mom and Dad's back, but I know how the old man can be sometimes. You deserve a chance to get out on your own a little. Cherry picking's no pick nick [joke!]. You have to work like heck to make any money at it. Most of the owners are real decent but some of them aren't. Go to the Chamber of Commerce right downtown as soon as you get there and ask them. They'll tell you all you need to know to get started. There may be a few guys waiting there same as you. Ask some of the older ones who've picked before which orchards are best and which ones to stay away from. I got cheated at one of them. Their name was Lubeke, [if I spelled it right]. Their son would go around during the lunch break and steal cartons from anybody who wasn't looking. At least I'm pretty sure it was the son who was doing it. Whether it was him or not, a kid I got to know told me what happened after I quit that orchard. [I quit when they cheated me twice on my count at the end of the day.] Ignacio was from down in Texas somewhere. Him and his family were migrant workers who followed the harvests, picking tomatoes, etc. I called him 'Iggy'. He wasn't real big but said he'd done some amateur boxing down in Texas. He quit the

Lubeke farm a couple days after I did, and we both ended up at the same other farm. He said something pretty bad happened to the Lubeke kid. His folks found the boy lying in some bushes out cold. Iggy said the guy had a broken jaw and had lost a tooth. I had to grin while he was telling me all of these <u>details</u> [which I wondered how he knew all of that] because all the time he was telling me about it he kept absent-mindedly [I think!] rubbing the knuckles on his right hand. We got to be pretty good friends. Maybe you remember he was at our house for a meal the summer after that, but you were away at church camp I think. Boy, this letter is getting way too long! "Old war stories." Ha ha It would be good if you could get a buddy to go to Traverse City with you, but it would have to be somebody you can trust. Living in a tent brings out the best and the <u>worst </u>in everybody! Now for some more advice. You should buy a face mask, snorkel, and a good pair of flippers. You can go down twelve or fifteen feet, no problem. I know you're a good swimmer because even before I joined the navy we spent a lot of time in the old Carlson quarry. I sure wish I could be in on this, but it would be a long commute from Lebanon! Ha ha. Don't even <u>think</u> about trying to rent S C U B A equipment. You need some pretty intense training before you're able to be safe with that stuff. We had a kid drown while we were still in training there in Florida. More advice: don't tell Mom <u>anything </u>about diving, etc. You probably already knew that! Listen kid, the treasure is real! I can feel it. If you can find where it is and it's too deep for snorkeling, keep your mouth shut and wait for me to finish this job and get back to the States. I don't know how to tell you to use the map coordinates. If you ask at the Coast Guard station

there in Traverse City you can be sure somebody will figure out what's
going on and the treasure will be found alright, but not by you! See
what you can do, but keep a lid on it kid. We've got it made over here!
A real nice apartment, a housekeeper, car and driver, the whole nine
yards! I'll tell you more about how we're doing in Mom and Dad's
letters. Act surprised! Ha ha. I don't know if or when I can get another
secret message to you, but if not, remember what I've said here. I'm
diving every other day. The Water in the Med. is the clearest I've ever
seen. Jenny and Robin just love it here. I do too. Remember, my cut is
40% of the treasure! Ha Ha. Just kidding! –Junior.

X   X   X

*1.17.26 That thar preecher man sez youuns got a license corse we never
had none so he sed gimme 2 dollars an you kin do the license thang
some other time that is fine an dandee with usuns as we was rarin to git
hitched leastaways I was. So his woman comes in she not drest fer no
weddin Im thinkin but the preacher sez she be a witness whatever that
thar is wal stan up sez the preecher so we does an Roseen she starts
puttig litel Renay on the bench rite next to usuns. That chile mouth jist
terned down all the way an teers start rite in wal ol dum me mebbe not
so dum after all I jist piks the litel un up an holds her reel tite in one arm
Roseen shakes her hed but I knows what I is doin an held rite on to litel
Renay she be happee as a clam then an no misteak that were the easy
part. The preacher sez jijne hands an we done that litel Renays eyes
biggern sorcers at sich goins on I so scairt my ol knees jist a nockin
together like I sed onct bafor in this ritin. I not skeerd a much but*

I shor was now an no misteak. I don't hardly member what all that thar preacher man sed but finely he sez you kin kiss the bride. My o my I aint never kist no buddy ceptin Mam wen I jist a litel sprout back on the farm in Ohiya. Corse Miz Polly the school mam done that onct but then she ups an marrys that ere Rankin feller him with alla them 27 melk cows he allus bragging bout. He allus pikin her up after school with a fansy rig gots yeller wheels an all an a whit e horse to pull it with I hope he makes her melk 5 er 6 a them ever mornin an nite ha ha. How am I goin to do this hyar kissin Im thinkin I needn had to worry caws Roseen I tell ya shes the purtiest woman I ever did see in them stor bot clothes wal she jist ups an takes me by my head an pulls me rite down she so litel an kisses me rite on my mouth kin ya bleeve that thar wasn't no ways neer what the school marm done no sirree. Wal thinks I Billy shor teeched her somthin bout this hyar kissin bidness or mebbe twas the other way around ha ha. Wal sez the preacher man. Wal what sez I . You got a ring fer yer new misses Roseen shook her hed she all reddy to speak up wen I puffs out my chist liked the ol red rooster an sez corse I does I fished in my poket an thar twas. A litel too big but shor sparkle some on that finger a hers she got some teers then an jist squoze my arm till it almost hert then a cors I reeched in the other poket and slips that thar litel doodad like a litel hart aroun Renays neck she laffs an trys to eat it ha ha So weuns is hitched all proper an ever thang. We was hardlee left the church house wen Roseen sez we gots to git that license thang tamarra she reel smart an like I sed the putiest gal I ever did see an no misteak about that no sirree. 1.18.26 no ritin taday. Got the license tho. 1.19.26 no ritin taday neether 1.20.26 Roseen rite wen she sez we needs better diggings so we hired a rig an went on down to Sheboygan town.

Musta bin 14 er 15 mile down thar tuk usuns all mornin even with a erly start like we done caws of the snow. Litel Renay cutern a litel bug her eyes jist poppin rite out at everthang something bothern me sez I what that be Roseen sez she was holdin my hand inside a my ol loggin mittens. Wal sez I how come them church fokes rung them church bells wen we was gittin hitched up an you kissin me on my mouth an all why was that enyhow I ast. Youd not bleeve what happen next they warnt no church bells rung atall she sez then she ups an kisses me on my mouth agin fer a long time the horses not needin any atensshum rite then. Wal you kin bleeve it er not but I herd them bells agin an usuns a good 3 mile outn Mackingnaw town don't keer ifn you bleeve that er not its true jist the same. She my litel darlin I never bin happiern rite now cant wait fer Mam an Pap to see us 3 an no misteak. You allus goin to be luggin that thar long gun aroun Roseen asts me Wal no sez I whar I goes Paps ol gun goes along with me never know when ya mite be needin pertekshun corse I knowed alla the time that gun never gon to shoot agin with them musket balls rammed down over that thar map a mine. Mite scare som buddy it bein big nuff that's shor. I aimin to git that peece home whar I kin fish that map out bafor it gits ruint. What is I aimin to do with it then the map I means I aint sartin. Roseen jist smiles at me an I be moren reddy to hear them church bells agin ha ha

X   X   X

"He really believes there is a treasure. That makes me feel pretty good about this summer," Tom whispered, handing Junior's letter back to Ed. The study hall monitor tapped his pencil on the desk where he sat, and gave them a dirty look over the half glasses perched on his nose. "See you right after school, o.k.? You still driving every day?"

"Nope. I think Dad smells a rat since I rode the bus today. Tonight I'm going to tell him I got dropped from the team. It'll be hard to get to drive much then, but I just can't risk him finding out some way. If he learns I've been driving when I didn't need to it would be the end of our trip this June, that's sure!"

"What about buying that snorkel and stuff? There's probably no place around here where they'd have that kind of stuff is there?"

"Not that I know of. I'll bet they'd have all of that in some big sporting goods store. Maybe Toledo. What do you think?"

"I've got an aunt who lives close to Toledo."

"Really? Don't you need to go there for a visit? After all, she is your aunt and everything," Ed grinned hopefully.

"Not in this life! She's the nastiest thing you ever saw. I wouldn't go see her on purpose even if she had our treasure buried in her back yard!"

"Well we've got to get that equipment before we go this June. You got enough money for your set?" Ed asked him.

"Not *me!*" Tom said, shaking his head violently. "I'm telling you right now I'm not doing *no diving. None!* I can swim a little but I don't like even being on top of the water, let alone down under it. If I have to dive with you I'm pulling out."

"Hey pal, no problem. I'll do the diving. That is if we are lucky enough to find the wreck and it's in water shallow enough to dive on without air tanks. *And* if I can get the mask and fins!"

"Remember that." Tom said, giving Ed the eye.

On the school bus that afternoon he dreamed up a plan, which, he assured himself probably wouldn't work. Staring out of the window as the bus jolted its way from one household to another, he hardly heard the racket from the kids surrounding his seat. "It's worth a try anyway," he thought glumly. "I've got to have that stuff Junior told me about, and it's only two weeks till June." Rain pounding on the bus roof and trickling down the windows didn't help his mood much.

Special care and a few extra jobs with chores were calculated to put his dad in a better humor. It didn't seem to work, but right after supper, when Calvin was settling into this favorite chair, Ed plunged in anyway.

"Dad, do you remember what a good swimmer Junior was before he went into the navy?"

"I'll say I do!" Ed's father perked up, lowering his newspaper. "I used to watch him in the old National Stone Quarry. Why he'd dive off those ledges and down he'd go. Scared the heck out of me sometimes. Thought he was never coming up! Then when I was about ready to jump in myself, here he'd pop right up, twenty or thirty yards off from where he dove in! I never could get used to such shenanigans, but it was something to see alright!"

Before he could raise the newspaper again Ed took the next step. "You know Dad, when Junior was home that last time he was telling me how much fun you and him used to have over at the quarry. He said sometimes he could see some really nice fishing lures stuck on the ledges down in there."

"He probably could at that." Calvin had forgotten the newspaper and was leaning forward in his chair. "I've left three or four in there myself. I remember losing a red and white spoon in that quarry once. Cost me two bucks. Man was I mad!"

Ed had his "fish" on the line. Now it was time to set the hook! "You know Dad, Junior said they're making a thing called a 'snorkel' now. You use a face mask with it, and you just have this tube thing in your mouth. You can swim along looking down, and when you see something you want to dive for, that snorkel closes up somehow and down you go. He says they also sell big long 'flippers' as he calls them, so you can swim a lot faster and go down deeper."

"Well Junior knows all about that stuff I suppose." Calvin was losing interest in the conversation.

"Dad," Ed said, closing in for the kill, "you know what? Junior will be coming back to the States in a year or so. Wouldn't it be great if you and him could do some snorkeling in the quarry? You might even find that spoon you lost, and maybe even some more lures and stuff. I'll bet that would suit Junior just fine!"

"Say, that's a real good idea Eddie," [he hardly ever called him that] "the trouble is though I don't know any place around here where

I could buy that sort of thing."

Before his dad could raise the paper again, Ed plunged in. "I'll bet there are stores in Toledo that would carry them. You know, like sporting goods stores."

"Maybe you're right. That would be *something!* Me and Junior swimming together again. You could come too," he added lamely. The paper forgotten he sat forward, staring into space.

"Hey Dad, they have the Toledo Voice newspaper in the library at school. What would you think if I was to look at their ads? Maybe I could find a big sporting goods store and we could write to them."

"Listen son, you find the name of a store like that and I'll just call them up. If they got any of those snarkles, or whatever they're called, we'll run up to Toledo and buy a set. How about that?"

"That's great Dad. Junior will sure be glad if we, I mean you, can get rigged up with that stuff. I'll see what I can find in the paper."

Ed could hardly wait to tell Tom!

X   X   X

1.21.26 Lookin fer a nice place fer usuns Roseen kinda pertikler whar we ends up usuns in a roomin hous rite now till better diggings I rekon1.22.26 Nothin she like yet not much houses to look at so many Swedes Frenchees an sich needn places to stay jist like weuns do. This Sheboygan town jist a hoppin 2 big lumber bidneses goin strong ol

Avery coulda sold alla our timber rite hyar Im thinkin. Timber comin by train kin you bleeve that? Roseen takes litel Renay all bundeled up like a litel exkimo an off they go lookin at lodgins she mitey pertikler like I sed but I sez you do that thar caws me Im tryn to find some werk. Got me a job taday still livin in a roomin house not neer as nice as that un in Mackingnaw town hope weuns kin git setteled purty soon litel Renay gots a cold er such not my wife so far caint git used to sayin that thar hardly but a reel nice sound to it an no misteak. Got hired at a litel mill the bigun jist laffed sed theys lots a men wantin werk but I sez they caint handel timber like I kin that cut no ice tho at that thar reel big bidness but the litel one took me on. They gots only 5 werkers 2 of em not werth the powder to blow em up. Boss reel nice a Sweed an a litel hard to unnerstan his talk but reel nice like I sed dont pay much but it helps an our monee hers an mine goin down as you mite expeckt. Don't know why I keeps on scribblin in this hyar diary a mine but jist kinda used ta doin it I rekon Roseen sez its nice to do an litel Renay trys to eat my pensil ha ha1.23.26 Bout the same taday. Like my werk remines me a loggin days up in the big woods Renay bout over her cold sure wish weuns could find something purty soon its too crowdy in that thar litel roomin house room 1.24.26 Blizzerdin taday I harlee made it thru that wind an snow you couldn hardlee see I lookt like Sandy Claws sez them at the mill when I finely got thar one of them 2 no goods quit taday boss glad of it sed I did more werk than them 2 by my self you think that didn make me feel good shor did yessir it did. 1.25.26 Nothinh new boss sez I kin help buyin timber I am purty good at it Ifn I do say it my own self 1.26.26 Pensil broke but Roseen rapped it up in some goods an it goods new nearly. Shes a treasure an thats a fackt me Im hearin them church *bells reglar haha 1.27.26 Finely found a place its upstars but Renay she loves crawlin up an down we gots 2 rooms up thar no heet but we keeps the door open on them stares at nite so long as they got heet on the bottom floor we gets by. Them fokes is French an Roseen tikled about that she goes down thar to do her cookin while us mens gone off werkin. You never herd sich talkin in that thar French tung as them 2 does I never herd her talk it bafor but she kin shor palaver in that thar silly soundin talk. 1.28.26 That Roseen she a treasure an no misteak she an them down first floor hit it off rite a way me an the man gits along too but caint hardlee unnerstan one another friendly though he is an I am too. Roseen figgerd out somthin them Frenchies gots a litel boy near litel Renays age so Roseen sez that French woomin caint never remember her name it somthin like Tonet er some sich. Roseen sez if that thar French woomin take keer a litel Renay alonga her own young'un then Roseen could look fer a job a werk. I dint want that Rossen a real sweety but she gots her own mind on thangs an thats shor certain. 1.29.26 No new thang taday septin Roseen out huntin week like I sed I don't cotton to her adoin that thar but she jist rassels my ol cerlee hair an kisses me on my ol mouth an I tells you ifn she tole me to jump in the crick Id jist say how soon should I do it haha 1.30.26 she done it shor enuff. Gots a job a werk in a bakry purty neer like she done at Mackingnaw town only goes mornings I gots no idee how much monee she be payin that French woomin name a Tonet er somthin sins they do all there palverin in that French talk dont matter none I gess she goin to do thangs as she sees fittin no matter*

*what ol dum me sez neether. Im lernin to let my Roseen do purty much
as she sees fittin an glad to do it too.*

X   X   X

"Can I help you gentlemen?" Ed was not happy that the clerk was
a girl. He knew his dad very well and he knew it would have gone better
if a man was behind the counter. "Country's Best" sporting goods store
was huge, displaying everything you could imagine for the out-of-doors.

"When we called last week someone said you carried snorkeling
equipment," Ed quickly replied.

"We certainly do. We just got a big shipment in. Swimming will be
popular before long. Tell you what. Go over to that far corner of the
store and I'll get Chris to help you." Ed breathed a sigh of relief, but
when they got there it turned out that Chris was a girl too!

Calvin was uncomfortable with the whole thing. First of all he'd
never been in a sporting goods store in his life. Of course Ed hadn't
either, but new things were easier for the son.

"We've got a son who's a diver," Cal blurted out. "He was a Navy
frogman in the war. Maybe you don't know what they are. Frogmen I
mean," Cal blundered on.

The clerk smiled at the two of them. "Oh but I do. I was engaged
to a boy who took that training just like your son must have. They

were all *heroes!*"

"Did he go overseas?" Ed asked.

"Yes. He saw lots of action but he was killed on one of the landings."

"Oh, I'm so sorry to hear that," Calvin said. "I'm sorry I had to bring that up."

"It's alright," she said quietly. "I'm married now and it's all in the past, thank heaven. Now, what are you interested in? How can I help you?"

"Our son, the diver . . . Oh, sorry! Anyway we want to see some of your snarkliing equipment."

"It's *snorkeling* Dad," Ed whispered.

"Oh, yeah. Sorry miss. Whatever it's called that's what we want to see. You got that sort of thing, do you?"

She laughed. "Sir, we just got in a shipment from our supplier. That underwater merchandise is really getting popular. By the middle of the summer you probably couldn't find snorkeling equipment anywhere. That stuff just seems to fly off the shelves! Probably what happened in the war had a lot to do with it."

She brought out several boxes and began opening them on the counter. "Is this for Dad or son?" she asked with a grin.

"It's for me, but maybe the boy could use it some too," Calvin said, now very much in charge.

"Here try this on," she said, handing Cal a red plastic snorkel. "We'd rather you didn't actually use the mouthpiece, of course."

Calvin was embarrassed. "Here, you do it," he growled, handing Ed the apparatus. The clerk helped the boy slip it over his head. She held the mouthpiece near his lips and explained how the whole thing worked. Calvin was watching closely.

"There are three different kinds of face masks," she went on, opening several more cartons. "Since I'm assuming you want this for casual recreational use only, the less expensive models would probably be fine. They'll do the job and they're built to hold up well. Now for the flippers. I've probably sold forty or more snorkels and masks during the last two years. In about half the cases the buyer said they didn't need the flippers. Well I can honestly tell you that almost every one of them who said that, came back in here and bought flippers. Until you actually use these you just can't tell what a tremendous difference they make. Again the more reasonably priced models would work well enough I'm sure. Now sir if you'll remove on shoe we can determine the proper size."

Calvin turned brick red, but he sat down and pulled off one of his "Sunday shoes". There was a small hole in his stocking. He grabbed the proffered flipper, jammed his foot into it, and said, "These'll be just fine!" Ed groaned within himself. His dad's shoes were at least two sizes bigger than his own!

"Those are the most expensive ones. If you'd like to try some of the more moderately priced . . ."

"I'll take the top of the line on all three things," Cal interrupted. "Nothing's too good for our Junior!" he remarked, jabbing Ed in the ribs.

"Your father certainly thinks a lot of you, young man." Neither Ed nor his father said anything then, but Calvin had a sheepish look on his face.

"What do I care who he bought this stuff for." Ed thought. "I not only snookered him into buying the equipment but it's the best they've got!" But he did care.

A quote from his American literature book came back to him; "If you want to make pigeon pie you must first catch the pigeon!"

X   X   X

1.31.26 No werk taday Roseen tell me she an the French woomin downstars an her man off to church. Me left with the litel French chile and Renay wich sutes me jist fine Renay allus watchin me ritin in this hyar litel diary a mine an trys to git them litel hans on my pensil so I finds a little stick a wood an witteld her one looks jist like mine an she rite off puts a end in her mouth it was kleen enuf Im thinkin but Roseen gimme hale Columbia wen she gots home. She warshed it reel good an gives it back to the young'un she be cryin fer it an all it warnt sharp on the end of it I knoed bettern that I tol Roseen. Bleev it er not she jist kist me rite in front of that thar French woomin she bout laffed her head off the French woomin did. 2.1.26 got all the way to werk an the boss sez no werk he sez everthang froz from the awful cold that come last nite so back to are diggins I goes it be good to be home a day shor enuf but thatl mean less monee come payday. The bakry never shuts down so Roseen off to werk in mornins only. 2.2.26 Same as yestiday no werk coldern a Exkimos but the Sweed sez the boss I mean. I tol Rseen what that thar Sweed sed was so funnee she dint think it funnee atall she tol me never to say bad werds in front a litel Reneay I sez Renay not old enuf to tell what that werd ment warnt reel bad any how but I wont do that thar no more an no misteak on that 2.3.26 thawed a litel las nite so werkin hard to make up fer loss time. Me an the Sweed gittn to be frens all most wisht I could ast him an hisn to come fer a dinner er somthin but no room fer sich in our diggins an no misteak on that.1 other no good werker quit yestiday so wes a litel short but the boss he pitches rite in to help an we gits her done. Wisht we could hire a nother man er 2 but boss sez cant pay em the big mills takin lotsa are bidness away from usuns. Roseen she a tresure an no misteak on that ya wouldn bleev what she ups an done wal I tells ya she bin savin her monee thats monee from the bakry ya see an sez rite out why don't weuns all go eat in a restrant Sunday next. I thinkin she meens jist us three no that aint it atall she and the Frenchie woomin names Tonet er somthin her man name a Jack only he sez it like Jock them womens been palverin around an gits a bee in there bonnet Roseen tell me to ast the Sweed if he an hisn wants to go too he gots no children jist a wife sickly she is. Them Frencheis down stars goin fer shor we to take the yunguns *rite a long Roseen sez. I thinkin not sich a good idee them young'uns goin too but whar we put em iffen we don't take em Roseen sez she reel smart Roseen is that's shor. 2.4.26Ya think that Sweed aint happee to be ast to go fer vittels at a reel restraant Sunday next then you gots a nother think comin so it all planned out so fer as me an Jack knows them women runnin the whole shootin match on this hyar restrant bidness. Me an Jack an the Sweed he named Swensen er somthin but he likes to be called jist Sweed better an I do too so Sweed it is I rekon. His wife mate jist reel nice but pale as kin be an cawfs somthin awful some times. Weuns had a reel swell time at that thar restrant even if litel Renay did fuss some till Roseen gives her a craker she brot in her poket book now whod a thot of that thar not old dum me that's shor Renay kinda makes a litel mess with that thar craker but it shet up her trap an no misteak. Sweeds woomin dint hardlee eat nothing atall but she jist kep smiling an makin a fuss over them 2 younguns you could tell she jist a achin fer a chile a her own onct I seen a teer in one a her eyes but she swiped it up reel quick. After that dinner cost me a doller an six bits fer alla us no charge fer the young'uns we all went to Sweeds to talk an sich since them rentin a house all there own he the Sweed tried to pay fer alla our dinners but we wouldn't hear a that. We gots monee an I guess them French got some too shor had a good time but I kin see Roseen worryin in her mind about that thar woomin a the Sweeds tell the truth I a little worryin my own self. That thar woomin pale as a white sheet an thinner than a fens rale an no misteak neether.*

CHAPTER TEN

Heading North

"Who's he talking to?" Calvin asked, looking up from some bills he was going through.

"Eddie's reading Eli's diary aloud, Cal. He says it's easier to follow that way. I tried it myself and Eddie's right. Do you want to hear some of it?"

"I don't think so. I tried reading some of those pages the boy is copying for Junior, but I don't have the patience for it. That old guy sure couldn't spell, and I can't for the life of me understand what he had against *punctuation!*"

Laughing, Beth said she had to agree. "I really enjoy reading those pages," she said. "Eddie's being really careful to get everything down just the way my great-great grandpa wrote it."

"He still sending those pages over to Lebanon?"

"No, it's too expensive by airmail, and we're afraid to trust sending them any other way."

"Well why is Junior so interested in that stuff? I can't see what a bunch of bad spelling and worse grammar written a hundred years ago can be of any interest to him."

"I don't either, dear, but maybe it's a way to think about home. I sure wish they'd get back to the States before long. The child will be half grown up till we see them again."

"Ed! That noise you're making is getting on my *nerves!* If you have to read that stuff out loud then go on upstairs. I'm trying to work on these bills and I can't concentrate with that mumbling going on and on."

"Sorry, Dad. Mom, I'll be up in my room if you want help cleaning the cream separator."

"I haven't run it yet Eddie. Thanks. I'd like to read the latest pages as soon as you finish them, o.k.?"

"I hear you quit sending those pages to Junior over there in Lebanon," Calvin yelled up the stairs. He'd finished stacking up some of the bills he'd been working on.

"No, Dad. Mom and I figured you'd think it was too expensive to send packages like that way over there."

"*Too expensive?* Why I remember your mother sending all kinds of cookies and stuff overseas when Junior was in the service. He likes to read those silly things does he?"

"He certainly does," Beth chimed in. "While Eddie was still sending them to him down in Louisiana he always said how much he enjoyed reading the 'translations'. That's what Eddie calls them; 'translations of Eli's diaries'."

Sitting down once more, Calvin lowered his voice. "Then tell Ed to package them up real good and send them off whenever he gets a batch done. Junior and his wife probably need something to cheer them up while they're over there. You tell Ed."

When Beth told her son what his father had said, he was not surprised. "Nothing's too good for Calvin Junior!" he told himself. It was something he could use again, and he had every intention of doing so.

Homework finished, he opened the diary and started to read. There weren't too many pages left to go, but that was good. Since school would soon be out, he and Tom would be busy getting ready for their trip. When he heard the kitchen door close he knew his dad had gone out to the shop. He ran down the stairs, feeling a little guilty that his mother was cranking the cream separator. He grabbed the handle, still keeping the momentum going. "Mom, when I go to Michigan could I take the diary along?"

"But Eddie, you said you were almost at the end of it."

"No Mom, I mean the other one. Eli wrote that one first you know. It would give me and Tom something to read and laugh about when we're through picking for the day."

"I'll have to think about it. Something could happen to that little book while you're up there. Those diaries are mine of course, but I have the obligation of passing them on in my family. Like to *your grandkids!*"

"Well for one thing, Mom, if I had the diary I might be able to find some of the things he talks about out on Beaver Island."

A look of alarm instantly crossed her face. "What's this about Beaver Island? You're not planning to go *out there* are you? I don't want that!"

Ed had made a bad mistake!

"Well o.k., but I'd take real good care of "diary number one" if I could take it along. Maybe I could keep it in one of those little round tin candy boxes you always use at Christmas time. The lids on those shut tight. It wouldn't be hurt at all. Think it over, o.k.?" The cream done, he headed for the stairs.

"Wait a minute! I want to know what you're thinking about that island."

"I'll tell you later Mom. Got more homework." He fled.

X   X   X

2.11.26 Aint rote much lately bin too busy with all the goins on I rekon so I gits back at it. Wal whatya think? Me the big boss man at the mill. Reeson I bossin tady wal Sweed he gots to stay home with his woomin she bein reel sick an cawffin bad too. Roseen she wants to go over thar an help Sweeds woomin but I sez no. it too far. Neer crosttown from our diggins to the Sweeds place an it cooldern a Exzkimos belly. See thar I bin cleenin up my talk ha ha. Nother thang I aint ankshus to see litel Renay gittin clost to that thar Sweeds woomin. Might ketch somthin her cawfin awful sometimes Roseen sez not. So how you so shor I asts her. Wal my litel brother dyed from that same thang she sez so I rekon she knows. Wal youd not bleeve whats in her bonnet now er mabbe you would bleeve it ifn you bin reedin these hyar hen scratchins a mine. Roseen sez she goin to take litel Renay rite over thar an stay thar some days to keer fer Sweeds woomin. She sikly an him needin to do a job a werk at his litel mill. No I sez I dont want you ner Renay neether to go over thar. Prolly no thang you kin do ennyhow that pore woomin gonna cash in her chips bafor long no matter ifn you ner ennybuddy else watch over her. Wal mites well talk to a fens post fer any good it done. She jist paked some duds an sich fer her an litel Renay. She kin say daddee plane as day now an how I loves to hear it sed an no misteak. I to take em with me on my way to werk tamarra walkin all the way litel Renay cutern a bug in them hevy clothes. Roseen makin her mind up you mites well fergit it thats shor. 2.12.26 No ritin taday too quite round hyar. 2.13.26 Same as yestiday. 2.14.26 I to be the boss man taday agin. Sweed stayed home even tho Roseen thar too. I so tired werkin fer 2 er 3 all by myself so I go on home after werk. Them French downstars gimme a good supper. I jist fell into our ol bed it purty empty thout them 2 miss em both bad an no misteak. 2.15.26 Sunday no werk 2.16.26 I stopt at the Sweeds on my way to werk he cryin some an his woomin in bed Roseen lookin tired out an Litel Renay wantin me to stay thar with em neer broke my ol hart but I needs to do what I could at the mill me an 2 otherns all that's left thar now. 2.17.26 Our best werker quit taday sed hed got hisself a nother job. Whar at I asts him. At the Consolidated he sez hangin his head. I gots 3 younguns an my woomin spectin agin he sez. What kin a man do he sez hes rite enuf fer as that goes. He wants me to tell Sweed but I sed you go an see him yor own self an git yore wages due to ya at the same time. Wal I couldn blame him atall but he the best werker we had next to me a corse so I shuk him by the han an sed good luck to ya. 2.18.26 2 gennelmens come to the mill taday I knowed em seen em lookin thangs over a time er two asts some questons about how the mill doin but me I kep my ol trap shet then next thang they ups an offers me a job caws they planning to bye the mill. Sed I could be boss an a timber buyer along with it. Wal I tol them buzards to git offn the propity fore I kicked em offn it they jist laffed an left the propity. Found out after werk they went to see Sweed an he jist sold out to em. He had no choict I gess. 2.19.26 the worst day I seen sins we got hyar to Sheboygan town worse blizzard I ever did see blowin in from the northeast. Sweeds poor woomin dyed last nite Roseen an the Sweed rite thar when it happen litel Renay was asleep thank heaven fer that. I warnt sprized it happen fer I seen the rags with the blood on em Roseen tried to hide em from the Sweed but he seen em too. Roseen takin over bout ever thang at Sweeds house him bein no good fer nothing an who could blame him. 2.20.26 Febrary aready an it neer gone. Funreal tamarra wont be able to bury her groun froze down solid fer 2 er 3 feet but the funreal man take keer of evething. Sweed to get monee from sellin the mill so thangs be all rite fer him now. 2.21.26 Funreal taday Sunday weuns all drest in our best clothes I thankful Roseen seen to it we all gots desent clothes. I don't ast her how much a Billy's monee still left in her poket book but not too much I rekon. Roseen a litel fussed up not bein use to a Luthren church she done good enny way Renay all big eyes at the goins on. Sweeds leevin tamarra he sez goin to Minysorta *or some place hope its warner thar than this hyar Mishigan is Roseen sez I purty dum ifn I don't know whar is Minysorta it colder thar than hyar. Wal he gots peepel thar his woomin had told Roseen them 2 gots reel good an frenly even so it was jist a litel time they had together. Sweed give Roseen clothes from his wife an some Baby clothes in a litel trunk. They had niver been used atall sins Sweeds woomin unable to have any younguns. That was a reel sad thang an no misteak.*

X   X   X

"How'd your finals go, Tom? I suppose you aced all your tests, right?"

"*Sure I did, Ed.* You know me. I even answered a lot of questions none of the teachers asked," Tom grumbled. They were once again sitting in Ed's car at Tom's house. Cal had finally allowed his son to drive, since it was necessary to get ready for the trip. Final exams over, the true topic of conversation was their preparations. They planned to leave on Sunday morning, four days later.

"Got your list with you?" Ed asked pulling a yellow pad from his book bag.

"Right here. You go first Ed." They compared lengthy lists of everything they could think of that they would need. Ed had already jammed the big tent into the bottom of the car's small trunk. His Mom's two-burner kerosene cook stove on top of it nearly filled the remaining space. Two folding army cots, blankets, pillows and other such items were piled high on the back seat. Tom insisted on bringing a sleeping bag, even though it took up even more space.

Cans of food were tucked in at random, wherever there was room. Potatoes, apples, carrots, and even a head of lettuce rolled around between the seats.

"Listen, Tom, I aim to be at your place about 4:30 a.m. Be ready, o.k.?"

"Why so *early* man? It should only take us about seven or eight hours to get there you said."

"That way we'll have plenty of time to set up camp. Sure don't want to be doing that in the dark! I had enough trouble getting that tent up in our barn. Once we are all set up, maybe we can start picking the next day, see?"

"O.k. I get it. See you Sunday. Nine thirty you said?"

"Get out of here," Ed laughed, pushing Tom out of his car.

As soon as he entered the house Ed could tell something was very wrong! His mom was slicing potatoes and keeping her eyes down on her work. Calvin was sitting at the table, which was reason enough to set the alarm bells ringing in Ed's head.

"Tried to get around me, did you?" Ed's father, speaking quietly like that was even scarier.

"What do you mean, Dad?", Ed stammered, knowing full well what was coming.

"I ran into Tom's dad at the elevator today. He was bragging about how you *and his boy* were going to Michigan in June to pick cherries." He stood up and towered over his boy.

"Cal!" Beth said, an edge to her voice. Her husband lashed out, palm open. Ed's hat flew off, his head flailing backward. *"Cal!"*

Beth screamed.

"You're as bad as the boy!" he snarled. "You knew about this all along and never said a word. Yeah, you knew alright. Some wife you are!" He turned to the door, sending a kitchen chair flying against the sink, and left the house, slamming the door behind him.

The tears came then, but Ed made no sound. Holding the stinging side of his head with one hand he left the kitchen, heading for the stairs. His mother made no move to comfort her son, nor did she follow him. Had he looked back however, he would have seen tears trickling down her cheeks as well. She knew Eddie's tears were not only because of pain from the slap!

X   X   X

Not even a rooster's crow broke the silence as Ed slipped from his bed and tiptoed down the stairs. He ate some cereal and a piece of bread smeared with strawberry jam. He was not surprised when his mom joined him, speaking in whispers. "I put a bar of 'Lifebuoy' soap, some laundry soap, a dish towel, and a box of matches in your suitcase after you were asleep last night. And here's Eli's first diary in this cookie tin. *Please* take good care of it will you?"

"Gee, Mom, I never thought about soap and stuff. I wonder how many other things I forgot. Thanks for the diary. I'll take good care of it. Maybe I can translate the whole thing while I'm gone. There won't be much to do after work up there." He didn't tell her that he'd packed the remaining pages of the diary he'd been working on during the winter. It was sealed in bread wrappers and shoved inside an undershirt at the bottom of his suitcase, along with a blank tablet and the map. The snorkeling equipment was rolled up inside the tent.

"So you're going?" Both mother and son jumped at the sound of Cal's voice. "Remember this. You get in any kind of trouble and you get out of it yourself. I will not come if you call up, or if anybody else does either. You were lucky last fall. Judge Crites could have given you jail time. Of course it might have helped that I share-crop his ten acres. Here." He reached across the table and handed Ed a crumpled ten dollar bill. "This is *emergency money!* I expect every penny of it back when you get home. If you're broke, and that car breaks down, this is bus fare back home." He stalked off to their downstairs bedroom without another word.

2.22.26 *No buddy feels like doin nothing today jist feelin sorree an lonely like. Hardly feel llike ritin but weuns gots to be makin sum kinda plans er other no more mill werk fer me an Roseen lost her werk at the bakry counta she missed werk while helpin Sweeds wife. We gots a litel monee left but itl go faster than Spring thaw Roseen knows it too so I sez we gotta palaver on this hyar bufor weuns cleen busted fer monee. Them French downstars wantin to help but we sez no thankee weuns gonna make out jist fine. Wal we sed that to em but I thinkin mebbe not. Wal I knowed what weuns had ta do an that be hedin south down Ohiya way an my fokes farm whar we kin git along alrite till I kin find a job a werk that ol summer kitchen be jist fine fer us 3 even if it does need a litel fixen an prolly a new stove fer heet an cookin on. Its funny tho ever time I sez them thangs Roseen shets her trap titer a new boot.*

She wont hardlee talk about it atall that thar idee a mine finely though she tells me what shes feered of I shoulda knowed it bufor but old um me dint. Whar yore fokes go to church at Roseen asts me. Wal sez I reel proud like they allus goes to a litel white church not moren 3 mile from our farm not many   goes thar but everbuddy frenly an preechin fare to mjidlin seein as how the preacher man bout a hunderd yar old it looks like ha ha. That be it Roseen sez a reel worreed lookin on her face. Them fokes a yers never gon to take to me Roseen sez. Why not I asts her cawse I Catolick an Renay goin to be Catolick too that thars why not an starts cryin to beet the band an no misteak. Honee I sez reel sweet like thems gonna love you to deth an litel Renay too. Pap prolly clame that youngen fer a granchile first thang we gets down thar to Ohiya. An Mam wal you jist wait Mam a reel lovin kinda woomen . I feel bad cawse I never sed nothing bout my sister Marybeth she a horse of a nother color an that's shor she never gots a good werd fer man ner beest. She could be trubbel she bein sich a jellouss type a woomin 4 yars oldern me an bossy as a ol milk cow. Mebbe I thinks I kin hanel that ol maid but like I sed I never told Roseen bout Marybeth atall even so I knowed I shoulda done that thar rite off. Roseen sez she gots to go to Catolick church an litel Renay too wal sez I theys one a them kinda churches down Mayvill way mebbe 9 mile er so a big one too I sez you could go thar. Howd I git thar Roseenh sez why shors fire I be the one to take you an the young'un an jist wait in Paps rig till youuns come back outa thar an that be how we do it fer shor. 2.23.26 Usuns not talkin no moren we has to an that's a fackt Roseen skeered a goin down thar to Ohiya an Paps farm an that thar summer kitchen what needs some fixin up an a new stove like I sed bufor. Wal what we gonna do then I asts her an she starts cryin agin cours soon as she starts bawlin litel Renay does too an I cant never stan to see them 2 cry like that. Monee wont last long I sez what you thinkin weuns kin do ifen we don't go down thar to Mam an Paps I dint say nothin bout ol Marybeth this time neether.

Know I should but feered wen Roseen herd bout a crabby ol sister down thar be all she need to put her litel foot down hard like she able to do wen she riled bout somthin. 2.24.26 bin lookin fer werk all day dint tell Roseen that I even went to that thar Consolidated with my ol head jist hangin I be so ashamed to ast them fer werk. The boss man reel nastee too. Sed you had yer chanct so jist git outa hyar for I gits reely mad an throws you outa the door. Lookt some other places too but no buddy hirein now as spring comin an no loggin fer a while. 2.25.26 I tol Roseen what happened at the Consolidated mill she grabbed me an jist kist my ol face sed she glad I dint git no werk thar them not carin bout no buddy. Ifn you don't think she a reel treasure wal you got a nother think comin an no misteak .Dint find no werk taday neether. 2.26.26 Weuns not gittin no whar on what to do so I figger it be bout time fer me to git up on my hine legs an take over an say whats to be done. I ast Roseen rite out how much a Billys monee she gots left an she jist pored everthang outn her poket book an shows me she still gots 14 dollars and 50 cents left a hisn an I gots 21 dollars my own self. Her werkin at that litel bakry an me at Sweeds mill shor kep us goin but that all over with now so I sez we goin to Ohiya an Paps farm ifn they don't like Catolicks too bad fer em cawse wes goin fer shor. Roseen mad but that no dffernt than bufor she bein mad then too so mite as well git used to it sez I. What you think a that me takin over like that thar wal some times a man gotta do somthin rathern set around and grump leastaways that be what I tol my self. Roseen pakin up stuff but not happy bout it.

CHAPTER ELEVEN

Cherry Pickers

"Well, we made it!" Ed yelled as they sped down a country road toward the highway. There was a hint of rose color in the east, but it was still dark at 4:30 a.m. This early on a Sunday morning there was no traffic at all. Tom said he was going to try for a nap until it was time for him to take a turn at the wheel. He leaned his head back but was soon leaning forward again, too excited to sleep, even though he'd hardly closed his eyes all night. They sang, or you might say *yelled* some familiar songs. "You Are My Sunshine" was repeated several times until they finally ended up laughing.

Once on the highway the miles rolled away behind them as the sun rose above a low-lying cloud bank to the east. "Looks like we'll have some rain pretty soon," Tom said, craning his neck to see out the side window. "Hey Ed, do you think your car's sounding kind of noisy?"

"Noisy?"

"Yeah. At least noisier than it was. Maybe it's just my imagination."

Ed let up on the accelerator and sort of leaned forward, listening. "Could be. I sure hope not! We've only been gone a couple of hours. Hey, Mom packed a lunch for us but I didn't eat much breakfast. What say we pull over at the next roadside table and have a little snack? I'll check the water and oil then too. Don't think there's anything wrong but it pays to keep an eye on this old crate."

They finished nearly all of the milk, taking turns drinking from the two-quart Mason jar Ed's mom had insisted they take along. "Might as well finish it," Ed said, wiping his mouth on his sleeve. "Soon as the sun comes out it's going to go sour." Raising the hood, he checked the water. It was right at the top, but when he pulled the dip stick, he let out a whistle. Without saying a word he held it out for Tom to see. Only about one eighth of an inch was showing!

"You should have filled it up before we left," Tom said, frowning.

"I *did!*" They looked at each other in dismay. "Never fear," Ed crowed. "Dad gave me a whole case of it. Twelve quarts. We'll be o.k. I'll slow down from now on. I've been driving pretty fast. This car always was an oil burner. I suppose that's why Dad gave me that oil. Probably use less if I drive slower."

"By the looks of things you'd better make it about ten miles an hour," Tom said, joking.

They had a little trouble finding the State Park, even though it was clearly marked on the Michigan map. It was a little after three in the afternoon when they finally pulled up in front of the park office. The rain began the minute they stepped out of the car. The office was closed!

"Now what?" Tom groaned as they sat in the car listening to the rain drumming on the roof.

"I think it's going to let up pretty soon. What say we take a little tour around the town and see what's here? Maybe get us a malt or something."

"Great!" Tom agreed. They cruised the nearly deserted streets, found a drive-in restaurant and had ice cream. The rain continued. The park office was still closed when they returned so Ed suggested they take some of the small lanes that meandered through the park, watching for what might be the best place to pitch their tent. There were no tents in sight but they saw half a dozen of the little house trailers that were getting popular. Tom said they were called "travel trailers" and had small sinks and everything tucked inside. "Sure be easier camping in one of them," Tom said, thinking about the job of putting up their tent in the rain.

"Why'd you bring that *darned thing?*" Tom yelled as Ed dug his school book bag from the jumbled supplies behind the front seat.

"Don't worry! I'm all done with school work until September. I promised Mom I'd send her a postcard when we got here. She gave me about a dozen of them. I'll tell her to call your folks and tell them we haven't been eaten by bears or anything."

"You do that. I'm going to see what's on the radio."

The rain continued, but they were safe, dry, and happy with the start of every sixteen-year-old's dream.

Ed finished the penny postcard and dug out the final few pages of Eli's second diary. "Want to hear any of this?" he asked. But

Tom shook his head and continued fiddling with the radio.

2.29.26 Tryin to finsh up everthang hyar them French don't want usuns to go but they knows I cant find no werk hyar. Renay shor gonna miss the litel French young'un they allus played reel good tagether onlee some times they mite scrap over a toy er somthin but just thang 2 minnits later they laffin an happee as clams. Roseen gonna miss talkin the French talk downstars an miss there compny too I rekon I unnerstan that I gonna miss em too but that be whar it at an no misteak. 3.1.26 Stage coach leevin tamarra bot 8 in the mornin. Weuns all paked an reddy but nothing to do but jaw with them French wal with her an her young'un caws her man gone to werk which I shor wish I was too but no werk here like I sed afor. 3.2.26 Why you luggin that ol rifel gun aroun Roseen asts me fer mebbe the tenth time. I sez it goes whar I goes never did tell no buddy that pertickler long gun wouldn shoot fer sour appels caws a them 2 over size bulets I drove down the barrel. No buddy knows bout that thar map neether no siree I gots a idee a findin ol Caroline ifn she not too deep down in Mishigan lake prolly never happen but I knows theres treasure a some kind down in thar an mebbe I kin figger a way to git it. 3.3.26 that thar stage coche like to shake a person to pieces. Renay kinda sik prolly alla that shakin an bumpin the road bein purty ruff an the snow still deep yet. Roseen takes good kare a that youngun a hern I mean ourn ha ha that litel un calls me daddee an I reel glad a that an no misteak. 3.4.26 Stayed in a inn last nite coste me 2 dollars kin ya bleeve it reel good super an brekfust though slep all in one bed an luky to git that there bein a passel a travlers on the road it seems. litel Renay feelin good longs as weuns not on that thar stage coche never throwed up though than hevens fer that haha. 3.5.26 Cant harlee bleeve it back in Ohiya taday but still not to Mam an Paps place

wal could say my place too as I allus live thar with my fokes an
Marybeth still never told Roseen bout ol Marybeth shoulda thats shor.
Wal she gonna find out soon enuf an no misteak on that thar. 3.6.26
Thar she is are ol barn an out bildins we on a hired rig from the stage
coche stop at Millvill Roseen lookin mitey worred like I tryin to calm her
some but it not werkin. Renay asleep she still gots a tummy ake from
alla that shakin an thumpin in the stage coche. She a mitey brave litel
gal to tell the truth. I a litel oneasy my own self no tellin what the fokes
gonna think me bein marryed up an the youngun corse she aint reely
mine wisht she was. Planninn to dopt that youngun soons I learns how
to do it proper like. Roseen happee bout that doption but shor aint
happee to be hyar on the farm in Ohiya. The rig driver help us git are
thangs up to the house. Mam jist starin fer a minnit then runs out an
hugs Roseen she holdin litel Renay too kin ya bleeve it we not even sed
howdy do yit. She hugs Roseen an the chile seen the lay of the land rite
away. She no dummy like me is next thang she does sez come in come in
outn the cold which we done reel quick. Know what she done then wal
she rung the dinner bell hangin on the shed. Yore Pap cutting ice down
on the river with them Holdern boys sed hed come fast when he herd
that thar bell fer shor it not bein neer to supper time atall. Bet yore all
neer starvin Mam sez all reddy she gots jug a milk an some bread from
the box. Kin you come to me an have some bread an jam she asts litel
Renay. Corse that chile not movin a inch from her momma an me so I
jist picks her up an plops her rite on Mams lap an she never cryed atall
Mam knows jist how to treet a litel stranger like Renay. Roseen hardlee
knows what to do so I ups an tells Mam her name an jist a little bout
how alla this come to be. Set down an eat sez Mam an we done that

an I begins to splane everthang but Mam sez no yore gonna eat then it
be nap time fer litel Renay an her momma too them both lookin mitey
peeked like which they was too. Mam kep bringin moren more food and
we et it shor enuf litel Renay fas asleep on Roseens lap an Roseen eyes
kinda droopin her own self. Bring that chile in here Mam sez an off to
the bed room they went. She lays em both down an covers em with a
quilt they both asleep in no time atall Mam an me has a good talk an I
sez mosta how it been with usns up in Mishigin an Sheboygin town too.
Wal Mam jist squoze my ol ruff hands an cryed jist a litel bit. Pap come
in then all excited sed hed seen the rig from cleer down at the river
where he an them Holdern boys cutting ice. skeered him that some
buddy mebbe hert when he herd that bell a ringin. Wal son he sez shor
glad ta see ya home agin. Theres moren him as come home Pap sez
Mam pointin to the bed room door. He brots a wife an darter too an
purtier ones you never did see. They all tuckered out fer shor. After
supper we all gonna set in the parlor an hear what all went on these 2
years. Whars Marybeth I asts Mam she over to Becklys Mam sez. Takes
keer a the ol woomin her bein bedridden. Marybeth helps her til her
boys gits home from werk her man dyed a year ago come June.
Marybeth be here fer supper when the Beckly boys gits home. Wal my
gals never waked up atall so I gon to sleep rite here in this ol chair a
Paps. 3.7.26 Ritin this hyar bufor I goes to sleep on a rug next to the
stove. This hyar what happen taday. Mam fix a reel brekfuss fer alla
usns. Pap an Marybeth not goin to werk taday sins alla usns gots a hole
lotta ketchin up to do an no misteak. Marybeths mouth all drawed
down like she et a lemon but youd not bleeve what that Roseen done
she areel treasure an no misteak. She sez to Marybeth you shorly gots

most bootiful hair I ever did see. Sed that rite to ol Marybeth. She do have awful purty hair an thats a fackt it yeller as a stand a ripe wheat in the sun. Wal thankee sez Marybeth an even trys to smile a litel bit. Wal that Roseen she a wonder what you think she do next wal she jist sets litel Renay rite on ol Marybeths lap yessir that be jist what she done. Look at the purty ladys hair Roseen sez to litel Renay. Wal that chile jist ups an puts her litel fingers in them yeller kerls a Marybeths an sez purty purty. Rest of the day them 2 Roseen an Marybeth hardly never stopped talkin to one another. I seen Pap grinning behind his hand he seen how that litel French gal handled ol Marybeth an no misteak. Thangs gonna werk out fine and dandee I thinkin. Roseen shor to figger out somethin bout that religion a hers I jist knows it fer shor. Aint never bin so happee as rite now. Start on the ol cabin tamarra me an Pap to farm together. No more ritin I gess no need to no more sins we all usuns home hyar on Paps farm in Ohiya.

X   x   x

By the time the rain finally let up it was getting dark. "Think you can sleep in the car tonight Tom?"

"Listen buddy, I can sleep anywhere and any time. Anyway there's no way I'm gonna mess with that big tent of yours in the dark! Just wake me, say about ten or so tomorrow morning. I'm going to listen to the radio some more. Found a pretty good station. I think they said it's from Charlevoix. Good music and not much DJ chatter."

"Sure I'll wake you, but long before ten! I want to get our park permit and find a good spot for the tent. Maybe we could even get out to one of the orchards by noon or so. You hungry?"

"Nah, not right now. Hey Ed why won't my seat slide back any? I can't stretch my legs out."

"Because everything's piled up behind the seats. Cots, blankets, your stupid sleeping bag, food, all that stuff. At least you don't have the steering wheel sticking in your belly! You mind turning the radio down a little? I'm gonna try to get some sleep. Don't forget to turn it off after a while."

It was a long night. Neither boy did much more than doze off now and then. It was getting light when Ed came fully awake. "Hey Tom, you awake?"

'I'm awake alright , and I'm *freezing!*"

"Wow! It *is* cold!" Ed said, shivering a little. "How can it be cold? It's June for Pete's sake!"

"Well remember," tom growled, "we're way up here in the *great white north!* What did you expect, heat stroke? See if you can pull one of our blankets from that boar's nest back there."

They shared the blanket. Both fell asleep again, only to be awakened by someone pounding on the roof. It was the park manager coming to work. "You boys planning to camp are ya? Come on in, I'm open for business. Want some coffee?"

Neither boy liked coffee but they could stand it if it had plenty of sugar and cream. The manager poured each a cup. It was hot, black, and plenty strong, but they sipped it anyway.

"Going to picks some cherries?" he asked as Ed filled out the park permit.

"We hope to. This is our first time. I'm Ed, he's Tom. We're from Ohio."

"First time eh? Tell you what. You boys go on and get your gear set up, make yourselves some breakfast, then come on back here. I can help you get ready to get rich in the cherry orchards!" He was chuckling as they left the office. "Take number eight," he yelled "There's a picnic table you can use, and you'll be pretty close to the restrooms. If you eat many cherries you'll sure want to be close to that building!"

With two working on it the tent went up quickly. Ed fished the kerosene stove out of the trunk, lit it, and they made toast by using dinner forks to hold bread over the flame. They organized their equipment, leaving much of their goods in the car.

"Want to go see that guy now?" Ed asked.

"Might as well. He probably knows a lot about the people coming up here to pick. Can't hurt anything to get all the info we can. After all, we're real greenhorns!"

"Ralph's the name. Been park manager here for twelve years. It looks pretty deserted yet, but you watch. By next week there won't be an empty camp site in the whole place. Mostly migrant workers, but there's always some people who come for a couple days just to get enough fruit for canning and such. How long you boys planning to stay?"

"Maybe three weeks if everything goes o.k. We're not really sure yet though. We're going to the Chamber of Commerce today. They're supposed to be able to tell us what we need to know."

"The season won't last quite that long unless the weather is not good," Ralph said. "Well good luck to you. Camp's a dollar a week. In advance. Don't go to the chamber. All they'll do is have you fill out a bunch of papers so they can schedule you onto the farms. They'll put you kids on the smallest orchards that pay the least. I can see by your hands that you boys know how to work. Here's what you should do. Just drive out on the peninsula three or four miles and start asking at the orchards. Don't stop at the first ones you come to. They'll already have contracted pickers. Won't take you on. You go on now. Stop in here once in a while and let me know how you're doing."

X   X   X

2.28.26 Wal here I am ritin agin sed I wouldn but here I is doin it. It jist near sunup an ever buddy sleepin yit had trubbel sleepin some buddy snoring prolly Pap snoring so dern loud coulda woken the dead fer shor wal got to thinkinh bout thangs an that be the werst way ifn you wants to sleep. Hung ol Betsy the long gun on a couple nails in the summer kitchen yestidy tol no buddy bout whats in that thar gun barrel an wont neither. Still cant think a no way to git that thar treasure outn the

Caroline her layin on the bottom a Mishigin Lake clost to that ol island whar I was fer a spell an Billy berried thar. I ast Roseen one time did she wanta go to that thar island an see whar her man berried at. She sed she dint not now enyways is what she sed. She never tol litel Renay bout her reel daddee the youngun too litel to member him Billy I means. I sed I think shes rite bout not tellin the litel one not fer a while enyways. Would take a heap a monee to try to git whats ever in the Caroline that's shor. She layin on the bottom. Prolly need one a them divin suits or some thang. I rekon thatd cost 15 er 20 dollars fer that an passage on a boat out thar in the fust place. Wal that ol lake froze hardern a ol biscuit till spring thaw so keepin my trap bout whats in the barrel a ol Betsy hangin on them nails in the summer kitchen. Soons Pap gits up I aim to help with the chores then me an him to start fixin up that thar summer kitchen like I sed. Truth be told I kinda use to ritin ever day even so I cant spell fer sour appels an have no grammer either like the school marm Miz Polly sed onct. Mebbe I sed that onct bafor in one a my ritins I fergit. Wonder if the school marm happee with that jasper gots alla them cows to melk hope not ha ha. Wal snorin stopt an Pap gittin up so he be the one doin the racket like I figgered. Wal wal Roseen sneeked in hyar an jist layed down rite baside a me she a treasure an no misteak. Never bin happier in my hole life an that's a fackt.

X   x   x

"You can Park over there by those trees. You boys ever pick before? Don't lie to me because I'll know anyway the minute you get started. Get on the wagon. You two will be working on row nine." She started the tractor and pulled out.

"Man, she's tough!" Tom whispered as they headed down a rough lane. "Knows her business too, don't you think?"

"Sure does," Ed agreed. "She's not much older than us. Seventeen maybe? We better try to get along with her cause I doubt if she'll take any guff from anybody."

The ladders were nearly thirteen feet tall, wide at the bottom and narrow near the top. Only one leg was adjustable, which seemed odd until the girl showed them how to stick the long, thin third leg right through the branches. This made it easy for the pickers to reach even the highest limbs.

"Throw off some empty boxes and pile them up under this first tree. Stack your full boxes here too. I'll bring the wagon around about five or five-thirty for your count. You'll help me load up, then ride back to the barn to be paid. You get fifty cents a lug. That's what we call the boxes. If they're not full and *rounded up* you get docked! Don't leave a tree until it's picked clean. I'll be checking that you do, especially the high fruit. I'll come back at noon with drinking water. Hope you got lunches with you." She turned the tractor and headed for the next row of trees.

They struggled with the heavy ladders, each boy on the opposite side of the first tree. Trying to hold the pail and pick with the other hand made slow going. "Hey!" a voice from the next row of trees stopped them. "Put your belt through the bail. Pick with both hands."

"Thanks!" Ed yelled back as they both did as he had suggested. Picking improved dramatically as a result.

"Tom, did you bring a lunch?"

"Never thought of it, did you Ed? Guess we'll have to eat some cherries instead. We'll sure think of it tomorrow though. We'll be starving by five-thirty!"

Tom proved to be the better picker. He had filled eight lugs while Ed had only managed seven. The girl examined each box, making sure they were full and rounded up. The boys had soon learned that ripe cherries tend to sink down as the day goes on. It took nearly an extra lug to round up their boxes for the count. "You guys did o.k.," she told them as they stacked the lugs in the wagon. "I'll be loading on down the line, so you can ride or walk back to the barn."

"We'll *ride!*" the boys said in unison. Their legs and feet were so sore from standing on ladders all day that they weren't sure if they could even walk all the way back. The girl laughed. She wasn't surprised.

The work went a little better each day. They decided to set a goal of nine lugs each a day, even if they had to work through their lunch break. Paid off at the end of each work day, they were beginning to feel rich!

"We don't work Sundays," the girl told them at the end of their first week.

"Say, Carol, It's Saturday night," Tom said with a grin, "How about you find a date for old Ed here and we all go see a movie down town? What do you think?"

"No," she said calmly.

"Well what are you going to be doing tonight then?"

"Whatever it is, it won't be with either of you guys."

"Sorry Carol."

"That's o.k. Tom. You two go yourselves. Maybe my boyfriend and I will see you there."

Ed was laughing so hard he nearly fell down. Carol smiled a little too. Evidently she was used to such offers.

Driving by the town's only theater they decided there was nothing showing they wanted to see. Neither of them liking to cook, they decided to get hamburgers in town, then go back to their camp.

"Listen to *that*," Ed exclaimed, locking the car. "Where's that music coming from?" A large group of migrant workers had built a fire on the pond shore and were playing guitars and singing. "Let's go down there," he said.

"I don't know Ed. Maybe they don't want us horning in on their party."

They walked down that way. The people there nodded to them, but didn't ask them to sit by the fire. They chose a log a short distance away and listened for a while. Somehow it made them both feel a little homesick.

X X X

"What is that thing? You got cookies or fudge you never told me about?"

"Sorry Tom, no candy. This is the *first* diary old Eli wrote. I keep it in this candy tin so nothing happens to it. Mom would skin me alive if it got lost or ruined or something, not to mention what my dad might do."

"Let me see that thing. Kind of falling apart ain't it? Man oh man, how can you *read* this stuff? I thought I was a bad speller. Old Mrs. James takes off two points for every misspelled word on English homework. If she saw this thing, that old guy would be about a thousand points in the hole!"

"You said it! Once you get into it though, it's not too hard to read. Want to hear some of it?"

"Nah, I'm not really interested. Why are you copying that stuff down the same way it's written like that?"

Mom wants to keep the originals just the way they were written. I send copies to Junior over there in Lebanon. He likes to read them. In fact he's in on the treasure. I guess I told you all that."

Ed settled himself in the passenger's seat of the Ford and began to copy diary number one, as he called it. Tom had the radio on, leaning back with his eyes closed.

"I'm gonna take tomorrow off." Tom murmured, eyes still closed.

"You're kidding I hope!"

"Am not. Nothing says we have to work every single day we're up here. Why don't you join me? We can go into town for lunch, maybe go swimming, something *fun* for once!"

"Aw come on, Tom. Tomorrow's Saturday, then on Sunday we never work. We've been doing really great so far. It'll be two weeks tomorrow and we've both saved about forty dollars, even after groceries, gas, and stuff. Tell you what. Let's take a drive this Sunday. Make a day of it. Find a good restaurant. Maybe take in a movie."

"A drive? Where?"

"I've been wanting to go up to Charlevoix. That's where you can get the ferry boat to Beaver Island. You know, check things out up there. What do you say?"

"How far is it?" Tom asked. He didn't sound very enthuse about Ed's idea.

"Get the map out of the glove box," Ed said. Looks like about forty miles. That's not far at all. Maybe a little over a hundred miles round trip. I'm anxious to get some plans made to get over on Beaver Island and do some snooping around. I mean to find that treasure Eli wrote about."

"You still serious about that treasure nonsense, Ed? You *know* it's only a pipe dream. Why don't you just give it up and let's go home?"

"*Go home?*" Ed exploded. "Is that what you want to do? Remember what the girl said when we first started picking? If we stay until the orchard's completely done, they pay a ten cent bonus for every lug we picked. They keep track of how many, you know."

"That would mean at least another week. I don't want to stay that long. We made some money. Let's quit!" Tom was looking out of the windshield, refusing to catch Ed's eye. It was obvious he meant what he was saying.

"Well, this is a surprise," Ed growled. "I thought we agreed to stay for the whole season. Now you talk about quitting. What is it with you, anyway?"

"You go on up there to Charlevoix on Sunday if you think you have to. You gonna pay for the gas out of your own money? You sure better not pay for that trip out of the kitty. We both put money into that, but not for no *vacation!* You go on. I'm not going. And another thing. You can have all of my share of your famous *treasure!* You'll never find it anyway, if it even exists, which I doubt!"

"If you think you want to go home, how do you think you're going to get there? I don't plan to leave until I get my bonus, so I guess you'll have to hitchhike."

Tom yanked the car door open and started walking toward the

lake. Ed jumped out too. "Hey mister!" he yelled. "You come back here till this is settled!"

"Make me!" Tom was bigger and stronger than Ed. He was not afraid of a fight.

Ed walked up behind his friend and gave him a shove. "You're a *cheater*" he snarled. "Yeah! You were going to go up with me to pick for a *month.* Now it's only two weeks and you want to run home to Mama. Well . . . ." He got no farther. He found himself lying on his back in the sand, ears ringing from a fist to his chin.

The fight went no further, but neither boy spoke to the other all day Saturday. Tom, picking with a vengeance, filled a record ten lugs, hardly stopping to eat. Ed filled only eight.

Sunday morning Ed took two dollars from his wallet and tossed them into the coffee can which held their joint expense money. "That should pay for the gas I'll use going up there. Is that o.k.?"

From his cot, Tom grunted a reply, then turned his face to the tent wall. He would take a bus home.

CHAPTER 12

"Going Solo"

Ed parked in the lot behind the small ticket booth. No one was inside, but a note said to ring the bell. When he did, an old man ambled out of a house nearby.

"Help ya?"

"I'm just getting some information on the island ferry." The man nodded and unlocked the ticket building. He handed Ed a fancy brochure and left for his house without another word. Ed climbed back into his car and studied the document.

FROM CHARLEVOIX: ROUND TRIP DAILY BY BOAT FROM OPENING OF NAVIGATION TO DEC. 15, $1.00 EACH WAY. AUTOS; $3.00 EACH WAY. SUNDAYS AND WEDNESDAYS: SPECIAL ROUND TRIP, $2.OO FOR AUTOS. PLANE TRIPS: [WINTER ONLY, WEATHER PERMITTING] $4.00 ONE WAY, $7.50 ROUND TRIP.TAXI SERVICE AND CARS FOR HIRE AT GALLAGHERS GARAGE, RATE 15 CENTS PER MILE WITH OR WITHOUT DRIVER. BUS SERVICE DURING SUMMER MONTHS. BUS FROM ST. JAMES TAKES PARTIES FOR ONE HOUR RIDE AT 25 CENTS PER PERSON. YACHT FACILITIES: BEAVER HARBOR, AT N.E. POINT OF THE ISLAND. ACCOMMODATIONS: ONE HOTEL, CABINS.

He had a little over an hour before the island boat left, since he'd had an early start from Traverse City, too excited to go back to bed. When he got up, Tom was still sleeping or pretending to be.

Ed walked over to the ticket booth and rang the bell again. The man came out after a few minutes, but he wasn't looking too happy about another interruption of his breakfast. "Does the boat usually leave on time? And it says here that there's a special round trip rate of one dollar on Sundays, right?"

"I figure you *can* read, kid. You want a ticket or not? I don't feel like coming out here again!"

"Yes. I'd like a round trip ticket. About when does the boat return from the island?"

The man came out of the ticket office and handed Ed a small red ticket. "One buck," he said. "Boat leaves in an hour. You ever get seasick kid?"

"No, I guess I never have. Why?"

The man squinted beyond the dock at the waves rolling into the harbor. "Don't look bad here, but it's blowin' about fifteen knots. It'll be kicking up right smart in the big lake."

"No problem sir. Thanks a lot."

With an hour to wait, Ed took out Eli's diary and began to translate.

X   X   X

August ten. 1825. My diary startin taday hyar in the big woods a Mishigain. Funny thang me ritin in a ol diary book an that's shor. My name be Eli Ephraim Yoder Mam sez you take these hyar diarys an rite suthin in em bout ever day what would I ever rite in em I asts her jist stuff that happen she sez Mam knows I kin hardlee spell cat but I figger the school marm Miz Polly sez ifn you caint read a werd sound her out that's ezackly what she allus sez so I asts my own self ifn that thar werks fer readin words orta do the same fer ritin werds down so that be what I aim to do ritin them werds the way they soundin. Prolly not be too good but thars fokes kin re-do these scratchins a mine till they makes sense leest I hopes so enyways. Me an 6 otherns got on a sale bote in Dtroyt town an hedded north in the old Robert Spangler. Got the spellin jist rite offn the back end a the bote ha ha. Made a reel good passage the wind bein behind us alla the way up hyar to Mackingnaw town then on to that thar Mackingnaw Island then far to the north Mishigin woods 2 fellers sickern dogs seasick they was but I never cot that sickness prase be fer that an no misteak 8.13.25. Gots to our camp taday hadda hoof it soons we got offn the Robert Spangler clear up hyar to the camp not too bad I thinkin gots a bunk house an a good spring jist ouside the door a good stove in thar but shor don't need no stove these days it hottern a new hosshoe. Are crew purty good. Boss man don't allow no funnee bidness he nots big as me but any fuel kin see better not mess with that thar bossman Avery is his name he gots a little shack next to the bunk house gess he thinks he bettern us mebbe he is we gots to see bout that thar ha ha. 2 guys Red an Orval they allus raggin me bout carryin Paps ol long gun wal Pap asts me do ya wanta take ol Betsy along on yer loggin trip. Shor sez I Betsy what he calls her. Shoots purty good even if she does pull to the left a little ifn yer shootin moren 3 er 4 rods out. Jist hafta ame a little rite an you kin hit jist fine course you hafta know bout how much an all which I purty much knows. I lugged that ol gun an powder an shot all the way up hyar there mebbe some god huntin bears mooses deers wolfs panthers too so mebe ol Betsy ern her keep ifn I gots any time fer huntin which I prolly wont atall. 8.15.25. Rain taday jist stayed inside the bunk house 2 guys playin cards got to yelling an razin cane finely one a them name a Joshaway er some sich poked the tothern in the eye an them 2 neer tore up the hole durn bunk house. I aint atall shor this hyar ritin I bin doins what Mam wanted but then she did say jist rite down what happens so that's what I bin doin so far ennyways. 8.16.25. Nuthin happen much. 8.17.25. Sames yestiday but gonna start cutttin timber tamarra Avery sez he the boss man. I shor reddy tard a layin around this hyar bunk house it be rainin neer ever day ennyway. Ast the boss could I go huntin some time he sez shor ifn I not loggin but better not catch me huntin when I should be loggin he sez an he means it too an no misteak. 8.18.25. Only got 7 logs taday boss maddern a wet hen sez wes the wurst crue he ever did see rekon hes right at that usns fallin over the logs an each other to boot. Them horses Ginger an Tops knows more about loggn than alla usns tagehter. Rekon we git better at it purty soon. We better Avery sez. 8.19.25. some better taday not much though gots 9 boss man wantin 12 er 13 ever werkin day. Big log fell offn the wagon on the way back hyar an busted a guys laig bad that be the end a loggin fer him mebbe hes better off than weuns is ha ha. 8.20.25. Hard rain taday so loggin goin mitey slow Avery jist hoppin mad usns laffin at him when he not lookin. No buddy kin keep the ol rane from comin down an that's fer shor. 8.21.25. Snowed a litel in the nite kin ya bleeve it this shor aint Ohiya fer sartin shor. Them horses Ginger an Tops likes the snow even ifn it dint last long once the sun come up. Weuns reely done good taday gots 12 big white pines even so we short a man cause a that thar broke laig on ol Trempert I think his name was still done good though. Avery dint say nuthin bout us gitn 12. Billy sed he seen ol Avery grin onct but I shor dint. Ever buddy likes Billy he a reel nice man bout my age that be 19 er 20 I not sartin which I is. Mam would know fer shor a course.

X   X   X

Ed threw his notebook into the back seat, shoved the diary in the cookie tin, and sprinted to the dock. He was so engrossed in the diary that only the warning whistle from the ferry kept him from missing the boat.

The problem began less that fifteen minutes after Starshine left the harbor. Having never been on a boat of this size, Ed was thrilled as she bucked into six foot waves out of the west. He hung onto the rail an watched as spray flew completely over the bow. It was cold on deck, so he soon slipped back inside the small cabin. He sat down on one of the long benches and glanced at the few passengers. Starshine not only rolled from side to side, but rose and fell from end to end as well. Ed's stomach suddenly felt very strange. He tried staring at the deck between his feet. It didn't help. He got up and stepped out on deck again. This was not wise. Watching the bow rising and falling with every approaching wave was a bad mistake. He hurried back inside and found the small restroom. He lost his breakfast, and kept on trying to lose it, even after there was nothing left to lose!

Deathly sick during the entire one hour trip, he wondered how he would ever make himself get back on board for the return voyage.

He stumbled down the ramp and onto the dock at Beaver Harbor, thankful that the motion was finally over. He recovered quickly enough and set off to see the town. It didn't take long. Most of the buildings had been burned down when the mainlanders "invaded" the small island and routed the self-proclaimed "King Stang" many years before.

Suddenly the teenager was very hungry. The hotel had a tiny dining room but they only served lunch and dinner. At his next stop, a grocery store, he bought two candy bars but was shocked at the price of twenty cents each.

"You're on an island now!" the young clerk said, noting Ed's surprise at the prices. "Just about everything on here has to come in by boat or plane so that puts the prices up. Say, are you o.k.? You look real pale."

"I got sick coming over," he mumbled. "The lake was really rough. Never been seasick before, but I sure was this morning! I hate to even think about the return trip this afternoon."

"Happens a lot. This is a bad time to come over. Most tourists and campers wait until after the fourth of July. Weather's usually a lot better then. You going back today? Your folks come too?"

"Nope, I'm alone. Been picking cherries at Traverse, and decided to take a little Sunday vacation. Wish I'd stayed in my tent!"

"Want somebody to show you around while you're here?"

"Actually I don't have much money for stuff like that, but I'm hoping to come back in a couple weeks. Maybe I could take a tour or something then."

"I didn't intend to charge you. I'm bored and you're the first thing that might actually liven things up around here. Mom will mind the store for an hour or so. What's your name? I'm Janet."

They walked around the tiny village while Janet did a creditable job as a free tour director, commenting mostly on the history of the Mormons' years on the island.

"Are Mormons the ones who believed in having more than one wife?"

"Yep, they did back then. I think it was in 1848 when this guy named Strang came over here and started a colony. He called himself 'King Strang'. Had a coronation and everything."

"Did he have two wives?" Ed asked with a laugh.

"Would you believe *five* of them? Had fourteen children!"

"How do you know all this stuff, Janet?"

"Actually, I help out when tours visit the island. I don't like doing it, but you do learn a lot of Beaver Island's history that way. You have to."

"What happened to him? Strang I mean."

Janet motioned for Ed to sit beside her on a bench overlooking the harbor. "He got into politics, and was pretty important, here and on the mainland too. But people got fed up with him I guess, so one day a U.S. Navy boat pulled in. Strang started to go aboard but two guys shot him in the back!"

"Boy, they must have hated his guts!" Ed said, watching Janet's expression.

"There were a lot of prejudiced people back then I guess. Let's go down by the fishermen's huts. It's about time they'll be bringing in the morning's catch. Don't smell too good though," Janet grinned.

"No problem! I trap muskrats back home. They don't get the name 'musk' for nothing. So what happened to the guys who shot the king?"

"Nothing! I guess everyone was so upset with a guy trying to set up a kingdom in America that they just let the killers go. Of course that was back in the eighteen fifties. Wouldn't happen like that today."

They watched the small fishing boats come into the harbor with baskets of perch and pickerel to be iced down and sent off on the island ferry.

"That's about it," she said, back at the store. "Anything special you're interested in?"

"How far is it to the south end of the island?" Ed asked, sipping on a bottle of pop.

"It's about nine miles, but there's nothing much down there. That is unless you believe in *ghosts*," she laughed.

"What do you mean?"

"Didn't you read all the brochures and stuff when you bought your ticket? They make a big deal about our resident ghost down there on South Shores."

"Yeah? At the south end of the island?"

"They call him 'The Captain', the ones who claim to have seen him. A long time ago a ship went down just off the shore down that way. Everybody on it was drowned. At least that's how the story goes. Myself, I think somebody made up that yarn just for one more incentive to get tourists to come out here. Ghost stories always sell, you know!"

Ed was so excited he spilled his soft drink all over his shirt. Even so, he kept his mouth shut for once.

X   X   X

The minute he got out of his car, Ed could tell that things were going to be better. The cook stove was clean, the frying pan scoured out with sand, and their blankets airing on the little clothesline they had tied between two trees.

"Hey man, I'm sorry I slugged you. I shouldn't have done that."

Tom held out one beefy hand and Ed took it with relief. "How was the island? Find any treasure?" he asked with a grin.

"Fraid not! What I did find was that I'm no sailor! Got sicker than a dog going over, and almost that bad coming back. I've never thrown up so much in my life! How'd things go here? Looks like you've been doing some housework."

"Pretty boring here. I went swimming in the park lake. Water was still pretty cold. I didn't stay in long, but had a bath anyway. Sit down and tell me about the island. You want some pancakes? I'm cooking tonight."

The pancakes were doughy, but both boys had learned early on that complaining meant the complainer had to be the next cook. "You still mad?" Tom asked, pouring even more syrup over his hotcakes.

"Heck no Tom. Hey, we've been buddies for a lot of years. We've had fights before. Remember the time I hit you in the eye with a corncob?"

"Yep, I remember that. We must have been about eleven or twelve. I was in one haymow and you were in the other. We were throwing cobs at each other and I didn't duck in time. Listen Ed, would you hate me if I said I still wanted to go home? Lately I've just sort of got out of the notion of cherry picking and everything. I don't know what homesickness is but maybe I've got it. I don't know . . ." Tom finished lamely.

"I kinda figured you might be thinking that way. Our orchard should be picked clean by the end of next week. You're a better picker than me, so you'd get a pretty good bonus if you'd stay on for another five or six days. Remember, they give us ten cents for every lug we've picked up to the time the orchard's clean. I figure my bonus could be around fourteen bucks. Yours would be more than that. Be a shame to miss out on that kind of dough, especially since we're more than halfway there already."

"Maybe they'd give me my bonus early if I go home."

"Tom, you know they won't do that. You have to stay for the whole time. If you really feel like you have to go, it's o.k., but how would you get there?"

"I've been doing some checking," Tom answered eagerly. "If you'd take me to the bus station I could get a ticket home for only about nine bucks. I'd still have made some money. We sure haven't spent much. You could have my half of whatever money is left in the kitty."

"But what about the treasure, Tom? I got another hint about the wreck of the Caroline when I was over there. They say there's a *ghost* watching the place where that side-wheeler went down!"

"Eddie! *Eddie!* This whole treasure thing is getting bizarre. A treasure map, secrets in an old diary, now a *ghost* yet! Like I said, I'm giving you all the rights to my half of the treasure. How's that?"

"Listen, I don't believe in any ghosts for Pete's sake, it's just that the *islanders know about the wreck!* Probably even know where it is! There has to be something to all of this, don't you see?"

"Well I can see you're totally convinced, so I wish you luck. But me? I'm pulling out. If you don't want to miss work tomorrow I can hitch-hike to the bus station. Should only be five or six miles, but either way I'm going."

"It's o.k., Tom. Sure I'll take you. What time does the bus leave?"

"I have no idea," Tom answered. "But if you'll just drop me off on your way to work I can hang around town until the bus pulls out. That way you won't need to miss any time picking. O.k.?"

"Would you mind calling my folks when you get home? Tell them I'm doing fine and will come home *very rich* from cherry picking. But be sure you don't say anything about my trip to Beaver Island. Mom would worry and Dad would be mad."

"No problem. I'll call them, and keep the island trip under my hat. Hey, since this is our last night together, why don't you read us some more of that diary? It kind of grows on you don't it?"

Ed opened the cookie ten and began to read.

X   X   X

8.22.25 *Sunday taday so no werk. Avery sez all werk an no play makes Jack a dull boy wal I don't know no Jack on this hyar crue but mitey glad* fer no werk taday this hyar loggin is hard werk an no misteak. They's a litel dog runs around our camp no biddy owns him so furs I kin figger that thar dogs name is Sneeky. How come he called that I ast Avery. Wal everbuddy laffed an Avery sed I'd find out one a these days. Wal taday I is tryin to git my hands cleen ifn you never tried to git pine sap offn yor hands an gloves wal you gots no idee what a job a werk you gots in stor fer ya. Wal I was bendin over that thar warsh stand an all to onct it felt like some buddy stuck a nife in my laig jist above my ol boot. I turns aroun an theres ol Sneeky got a hold an bitin me like I sed. I tried to kick him but he lets go an runs off an hid hisself under the log pile ever buddy laffin they heds off an ol Avery sez now yall knows why that thar dog called Sneeky yessir I knowed all rite. Billy sed that thar dog done bit jist about ever buddy in our camp the sneaky litel devil. Avery gots two pals on the crue. Them 3 allus jawing bout somthin but keeps to they selfs what iver it is they be jawin about. Me I keeps my ol trap shet an minds my own bidness. Boss sez I kin go huntin taday bein it be a day offa werk so I went. Done purty good ifn I do sez it my own self kilt a litel yearling deer jist outa the camp a ways weuns gonna have deer meat fer supper tonight fer shor the boss sez. He shor never thankt me a corse. Towards evenin up comes a black bear a reel biggun too I shot but missed wal sez I he shor got the skare a his life ha ha don't know who was the skaredest me or that ol bear. 8.23.25 Wek goin good even ifn ol Avery never sez so I gess he has to be meen an tuff to keep a bunch a fellers like usns in line wal he shor does that an no misteak. Ever buddy grumpin bout the cook he don't know much about gittin stuff sos its good to eat. One a the guys grumped at the cook so he throwed a kittle a hot water rite on his face you shoulda herd him *holler the rest of us jist laffed it so funnee. Boss Avery asts do any a us otherns want to be the cook asts me too no sir Mr Avery sez I me would be worser than Zeb ever was an that's a fackt. 8.24.25. Werk goin purty slow bein as we short handed rite now boss don't complane much manely caws he not here most a the time. Him an them 2 that's allus hangin round him still jawin like bafor. Weuns does our werk but no buddy tryin to set no rekerds on cutting timber nor lodein it neether when the cats a way the mice will play I member that thar sayin from a Mguffee Reader I used to have on the farm back down thar in Ohiya. I don't think Mam er any buddy else gonna read this dum stuff I be ritin alla time who cares ifn we cut timber er not way up hyar in the big woods a Mishigin. Aint even no intrest to my own self not to say any buddy else but Mam sez do er so I do er mebbe she like to read these hyar dum werds an sich come an evenin by the fire side who can say. I shor miss Mam an Pap speshly Mams cookin an that's a fackt. 8.25.25. Nuthin new taday. 8.26.25 Boss man Avery bin lookin at me kinda funnee asts what tis I bin ritin in these hyar books I hadda show im a page er 2 but he still looks a litel suspishus to me. Gonna not rite fer a while hid the dirys in my ol tore up boot ifn he finds it I be in hot water an no misteak. Wal Wal used up ever bit a the pages in this hyar first book. Mites wal start on the new one. Mam be pleezed I rekon.*

CHAPTER 13

Wreck of the Caroline

Ed felt a little sad as he pulled away from the bus station. Tom was standing there by the door, but he didn't look up or wave. There was no doubt that the boy was homesick. It was best for him to go on home, Ed thought. In a way he was glad that Tom had left. His friend had made it clear that he had no intention of spending any time on Beaver Island. Since that was the case, it would have looked very funny to Ed's parents if he didn't come home when Tom did. "Well, I'm really on my own now," he thought as he headed up the peninsula to the cherry orchards.

"Where's your pal?" Sally asked as several pickers climbed onto the wagon. The work had progressed farther up the hills as each row of trees was picked clean.

"Had to go home," Ed said as they jolted their way up the hill.

"Where's home?" Sally asked over her shoulder. She was very much at home driving the tractor.

"We're from Ohio. My older brother did some picking up here before he joined the navy. He told me about it."

"You still staying in a tent down in the State Park?"

"Yeah. It's pretty nice, and doesn't cost much."

"You could put your tent up right in the orchard if you want to. There are three tents here now."

"No thanks," Ed replied as the wagon stopped. "I'm all settled there, and they've got restrooms and everything. Besides, won't be much longer until your orchard's done will it?"

"Should finish by the end of this week. Be sure to stay until then if you can. Otherwise you'll lose your bonus."

"I sure intend to," Ed said as he threw off a pile of lugs for his day's work.

X   x   x

In spite of himself, Ed found that he was missing his buddy. They had been friendly rivals in the orchard, taunting each other, as to which was the better picker. Sometimes they made bets on the day's outcome. Tom invariably won. No money was involved; just the loser had to do various camp chores. As a result Ed got to be a fair camp cook!

The days were long and the evenings longer, but Ed kept at the job, and his "grub steak" grew as the week came to an end. The last tree was picked clean by noon on Friday. The farm owner thanked the workers for staying until the harvest was over. Bonuses were paid, and in a matter of minutes the orchard was deserted.

Ed's bonus came to fourteen dollars and ten cents!

Heading back to the State Park, Ed stopped at a small restaurant and treated himself to the "blue plate special". Fried chicken, peas, mashed potatoes, bread, and milk. Desert was a piece of pie. Cherry of course!

He loosened his belt one notch, surprised at how thin he had become. "Man oh man!" he thought. "That meal was great, but it cost me a dollar and thirty-five cents! Add a quarter tip I left for the girl, and I had to pick three lugs of cherries just to pay for it!"

The job had taught Ed much about the value of money!

The rest of the afternoon was spent cleaning up around his camp and going for a swim and a bath in the little lake. The water was cold, but not nearly as freezing as it had been when he and Tom arrived, three weeks before.

He used the mask and snorkel again and was delighted at how much he could see under the surface. Fish came close and seemed unafraid. The only problem was the swim fins for his feet. As he had known, they were too large. Three pairs of work sox helped a lot. He had used the outfit four times and was gaining confidence.

Sitting on a rock by the water, he wrote another penny post card to his parents. Of course he told them nothing about his plan to go back to Beaver Island on the following day. "Tom better not spill the beans!" he thought. "Mom would be real worried and Dad . . .well I won't think about what he'd do."

Rain slamming against the tent roof woke him just before dawn. He groaned as he thought of packing everything up, especially a heavy, wet tent. It took most of the morning, and the back seat of his car was wet and gritty with sand.

Suddenly he slapped himself on the forehead in disgust. "How dumb can I *be?*" he asked aloud. "There's no way I can get to Charlevoix in time to catch the ferry today, and now I've got no place to *sleep tonight!* Stupid! Stupid! *Stupid!*" He sat in the car, enduring the smell of wet canvas from the back seat. Most of Tom's kit was jammed in there too, as there was no way the bigger items could have been taken on the bus. For several minutes he just sat and watched the raindrops sliding down the windshield. Finally he took a deep breath, started the car, pulled out of the park, and headed north. He had no choice. He would park in the ferry's parking lot and sleep in the car all night. He planned to be the first car in line the following day. It would cost three dollars to take his car to Beaver Island, and another three to get back. "Six bucks!" he thought, heading north out of town. "That's *twelve lugs* of cherries. Over a full day's work! Oh well, I'll never miss these few dollars when I bring up old Eli's treasure!"

He sang along with the radio all the way to Charlevoix.

There was no way to get comfortable in the front seat, but he finally fell asleep. Toward morning he had a dream. Actually it was a nightmare. He was swimming down and down toward a shipwreck that looked exactly like one he had seen in a comic book at home. Another swimmer was right alongside, and when he looked over at him it was his father, wearing a face mask and work clothes. He woke up breathing hard. It would be a long time before he would remember the dream as being funny!

In spite of the horrendous cost, he knew he had to take the car to the island. He still had some food in the trunk, so he wouldn't need to buy much while he was there. He could pitch the tent, so it wouldn't be too expensive once he had made camp. He was first in line to drive aboard. The assistant guided him into the bottom of the ship where it looked like there was room for at least eight or ten vehicles. Only two others came aboard.

Remembering his disastrous first crossing a week before, he decided to simply stay in his car. It was fairly dark in the ship's hold and quite noisy, but he did not get sick. "Made it!" he breathed as they bumped the dock on Beaver Island. He drove off the boat just as the clouds finally cleared, promising a beautiful, sunny day. He parked in front of the grocery store he'd been in before. An older man was at the counter, the girl he remembered was nowhere to be seen.

"Help ya?"

"Who can I see about a place to camp?"

"You mean 'whom' do I see don't you?"

Laughing, Ed replied. "I guess I do. You sound like Mr. Taylor, our English teacher."

"Not surprised. I'm the English teacher here on Beaver. Of course I teach all the other subjects as well. Sixteen students, grades one through ten. Bet that's a little different from your school isn't it?"

"Yes, it sure is! I'm going into grade eleven this fall. Are your students clear done after tenth grade?"

"Not hardly! We send them over to the mainland for their last two years so they can take subjects we can't deal with here. Usually only one or two kids each year. You want to know about camping you said."

"That's right. I can only stay for a few days, but I can't afford lodging."

"Ever do any camping before?"

"I sure did! A friend and me . . . I mean I, were picking cherries for about three weeks at Traverse City. Camped in the State Park all the time. He didn't come out to the island though. Went home yesterday. I've got a nice tent, and I don't leave any messes."

"Truth is," the school teacher/store keeper said, "you can camp about anywhere on the island except in town or on anybody's private property. Won't cost you anything out here."

"How do I tell if I'm on somebody's land? I was hoping to set up somewhere down on the south end of the island."

"You won't have any trouble at all down there. There's only one cottage and it's all fenced off. Retiree and his wife live there the year around. Name's Coleson. Lately they've had a kid down there with them, maybe a couple years younger than you. Now do you need any groceries before you head down that way?"

Somewhat reluctantly, Ed bought the few things he'd need, wincing at the prices. "Do you have any rope? Half inch or so?"

"Do we have any *rope?*" he crowed. This is a *fishing village* young man!
We stock plenty of rope, and sell lots of it too. How much do you need?"

"About thirty feet of half inch."

"Gonna tie your tent down are you? That's a good idea. Get plenty of wind down on the south shore. Quarter inch would do for that, and be cheaper too."

Ed nodded. He was not planning to use the rope on his tent. He had some for that already. "I guess I'll take the half inch anyway," he said. He wanted rope strong enough to haul up *cases of treasure!* Of course he didn't tell the man that!

X   X   X

There is nothing so unpleasant as a totally wet canvas tent, as Ed was finding out. By the time he had finally got the thing up and secured he had broken two fingernails. A steady wind off the lake was good news. With everything open it looked as if the tent would be pretty well dried out by time for bed.

He pulled the Ford around close to the other side of the tent, hoping it would help block the wind, which never seemed to stop. The waves rolled in and slid dying up the rocky shore. Ed stared out across the waves, a little troubled at the breakers. "How in the world will I ever be able to find what's left of the *Caroline* in all this water?"

"That your car?"

Ed nearly jumped out of his shoes. He turned to see a boy standing behind the tent, eating an apple.

"Yeah, it's mine. Where'd you come from? You about scared the daylights out of me!"

"It's really yours, not just your dad's or something?"

"It's mine. Do you live in that house back there?"

"I live there but they're not my parents. Mom and Dad got divorced years ago. Mom's all messed up or something. I don't know what's wrong with her, but anyway Grandma and Grandpa asked me if I wanted to come up here for the summer. Anything was better than seeing Mom so gloomy all the time and Dad . . .I don't know where Dad is. So here I am."

"Hey, I'm sorry. I didn't mean to pry into your whole life the minute you got here."

"That's o.k. I'm gonna get me a car this fall. How much did it cost you?"

Ed did his best to keep from staring at the boy before him. He was probably six inches shorter and a good deal thinner than himself. "You have to be sixteen to get a driver's license you know."

"Sure I know. Everybody knows that. I'll *be* sixteen on October seventh. Been saving my money. That's thirty-five Ford ain't it?"

"Yes it is. What's your name? I'm Ed Nolan."

"Earl Cramer. Grandma and Grandpa's name is Coleson. What kind of mileage do you get? Use any oil does it? If you're all done with your tent and stuff why don't you come down and meet my grandparents? They're o.k. *Really!*"

"Hey, I don't think . . ."

"Come on. You could have dinner with us."

"No! Wait a minute, I'm not invited, and . . ."

"Come on!"

The cottage was not fancy, but comfortable. The boy's grandfather was tall, thin, and almost totally bald. His wife was fairly tall too. They seemed to be "o.k." as Earl had proclaimed.

"What happened to your finger?" the lady asked.

Ed hadn't noticed that one torn nail was still bleeding a little. "I guess I got that putting my tent up. The thing's heavy enough when it's dry but it seems like it must weigh twice as much all wet like it was. It's drying out pretty well now though. I may use my sleeping bag if it gets real cold tonight," he said, silently grateful Tom had had no choice but to leave the bag when he left on the bus.

"Where are you from?" the grandfather asked from his chair by the stove. Ed gave them a very much abbreviated version of his summer.

"How in the world did you end up out here all by yourself? Good heavens there are nicer places to camp out, I would think," Earl's

Grandmother asked with a laugh.

Ed was torn. How much should he tell them? He had only met them an hour before. They may have even known about the *Caroline*. Maybe they were after the treasure themselves.

"I'm sorry," she smiled. "It's none of my business. We're just glad you came. Hope you can stay a while. Earl would enjoy some company his own age." Her eyes were kindly, her husband seemed trustworthy, and certainly their grandson would be no threat.

Ed made a decision.

"To tell the truth I learned about a ship that went down somewhere off the island, and I got really interested in the whole story. Maybe there's nothing to it, but since I had a few days before I had to get back to the farm I decided to just bring the tent and look around a little. I guess I told you my buddy, Tom, had to go home, so I came on alone."

Ed was astonished when all of them burst out laughing. "Why Ed, my boy, *everyone* on Beaver Island knows about the wreck of the *Caroline!* Why if you'd pitched your tent a hundred yards or so on down the beach you'd be right even with what's left of that old side-wheeler!"

For a minute Ed felt like he was going to faint. He gulped and grabbed a couple deep breaths.

"Are you *all right, Ed?*" the lady asked in concern. "You looked a little pale all at once. Earl, get him a glass of water. Hurry up!"

"I'm all right now, just felt kind of funny for a minute," Ed managed lamely. "Does everybody out here know about the *Caroline* then? It was a long time ago that it sank."

Mr. Coleson stood up and slid a small wooden box from under a desk by the window. He raised the lid and pulled out a dark brown bottle, intact except for the neck, which was missing. "Look at this," he said, handing the relic to his visitor. "Earl found this in shallow water just off the beach the first day he was here. It's broken of course, but I'd bet a lot that it came from the old *Caroline.* Did you ever see anything like it?"

"Now Frank, you don't know that. Some old French trapper might have had one drink too many and threw this bottle away. You and Earl just have too much imagination, that's all."

Ed forced himself to make small talk for another half hour, then told them he needed to get back to camp. It would be dark soon, and he still had some work to do before bedtime.

"I'll come with you!" Earl exclaimed, grabbing his jacket.

"Earl!" Carrie said. "You haven't been invited! Ed said he has some work to do before night comes. You might be in the way."

"No, it's o.k. I'd be glad for the company. Come on Earl, a cold, wet tent awaits us!" Grinning, they left the cottage and half ran down the beach toward his tent.

Camp work was forgotten. Ed got right to the point. "Can you really tell where the wreck is, Earl?"

"Sure! A lot of people, . . . well, not a *lot* really, but some of them that live out here year around fish right over the wreck sometimes. Don't catch much that I can see though. No one's been fishing out there since I came. Too early I guess. Water's still pretty cold I suppose."

Just as Mr. Coleson had said, the boy only had to lead Ed a short distance down the shore. "Right out there," Earl said, throwing a rock out over the waves. "I found that old bottle right beside that black rock. The one that's sticking out of the water. Got my feet wet getting it, and Grandma gave me the dickens. She's always afraid I'll get sick again. See I got asthma. That's partly why I'm out here on the island. I don't get it out here. At least I haven't yet anyway."

Ed was only half listening as the boy prattled on. It was obvious the kid was starved for company. "How deep is the wreck," Ed asked, interrupting the almost constant flow of verbiage. "Can you see any of it?"

"Not deep. I'd say eight or ten feet's all. Maybe Grandpa will let us take his boat out there tomorrow. We could even do some fishing if you want to. He's pretty particular about his boat though. It's just an old rowboat, but I think he's afraid I'd get in trouble trying to handle it by myself. Come to think of it, he probably won't let us."

"Man, you're a non-stop talker!" Ed laughed. "It's o.k. Don't ask."

Ed watched his young friend hurry about, doing his best to be helpful. It was somewhat disturbing that Earl seemed to be attempting to imitate Ed's actions around the campsite.

The younger boy's breathing seemed a little labored on this cold morning, but he did his best to hide the problem. "I wish there was something I could do for that kid," Ed thought silently. "I'll bet if I could get him back on our farm and put him to work for a summer he'd be a lot better!"

He didn't realize that farm work would be the worst thing for Earl to do.

"Maybe your grandpa will let us use his boat if he gets to know me a little better. Fishing's not my thing. Anyway, I'd need to get an out-of state license. I can't afford that. I'd just like to poke around the old *Caroline* a little. Want to give me a hand setting up my kerosene stove?"

"Sure! Just tell me what to do."

"I figure on stretching a tarp between a couple trees so I can put the stove under it. That'll be my kitchen. A few flat rocks will do to set the stove on."

Earl scrambled around, and was soon lugging two heavy flat stones. "These o.k.?"

"No Earl, we won't need to carry them all the way back to the tent. There's plenty of them right back there. If there's anything this island's got, it's rocks!"

It was barely light to the east across the lake when

Ed was awakened by loud coughing noises just outside his tent. He knew what those sounds meant! "Is that you out there, Earl?"

"Yeah. You up yet?"

"Not hardly! Why are you down here so early anyway?"

"I've got good news! Grandpa says we can use the boat, but only if he goes along. He's going to do some fishing if there are any there."

Ed's heart sank. He surely didn't want Mr. Coleson snooping around over the wreck, even if it was true that almost all the islanders knew about it. "How would he know if there are any fish out there?" he asked.

"You can *see* them! Mostly ring perch. Sometimes a few bass. Grandpa and Grandma say that perch make the best eating. May not be any out there, but have you seen how *calm* the water is today? Oh I guess you haven't got up . . where you going?"

"I'm going to the bathroom, Earl." Ed tried to keep the edge off his voice. After all, thanks to the boy and his grandparents he was going to get his first look at the *Caroline!*

"What bathroom?"

"See that downed birch log way back there to your left? I dug a hole under it. That's for number two. Number one is anywhere back in the woods, out of sight."

"Boy!" Earl exclaimed. In admiration, "You have *got it made, Ed!*"

"You might not have thought so if you'd been fighting mosquitoes half the night, like I was. Look." He showed the boy the red bumps all over his neck and ears.

"Grandma says you're to come for breakfast at our house."

"Gee, thanks Earl, but . . ."

"No, it's o.k. Besides, Grandpa's going to need some help launching the boat. I'm not supposed to do much heavy work. Sometimes it gets me to start wheezing. It's from the asthma." Ed didn't know what to say to that, so he said nothing.

Carrie seemed to truly enjoy having him at their cottage for breakfast. It was a real treat. Ed told her, laughing, about some of he and Tom's adventures with trying to cook.

"Haven't had her out yet this summer," Frank said, pulling a ragged tarp off the sixteen foot boat. "She's pretty heavy, but just what you need in these waters."

Using the log "rollers" stored under the boat, they had little trouble bumping it along to the shore. "No dock possible here. We had one once but the ice came in during the winter and busted it all to pieces. We don't use the boat that much anyway. If I get the urge to do some fishing I just hire a boat and guide in the village. We always get our limit. Earl and I are going to do that one of these days, aren't we Pal?"

"The wreck used to be in deeper water. When I first came here, about forty years ago, the lake was quite a bit deeper. The level of all the lakes has gone down some, so the beach is wider now, and the wreck is only about ten feet below the surface," Frank was saying as he rowed.

What little breeze there was didn't bother them. Frank knew how to handle a rowboat and it was less than half an hour until Earl was leaning over the rail, peering down at the bottom. "Drop it Grandpa!" he shouted. The anchor went over and the boat jerked to a stop. "Take a look Ed!" the boy grinned.

Face close to the water, Ed saw it then. It was now only a jumble of round stones and very old timbers. Here and there shards of rusty metal were visible too. "Is that it?" Ed breathed.

"That's the *Caroline.* It's a well-documented wreck so there's no doubt about it. See any fish, Earl?" Frank was baiting his hook with small yellow leaches.

"Yeah, Grandpa. There's a little school of yellow perch out that way." In less than an hour Frank had caught three. He then gave the rod to Earl who caught two more before the hook got snagged on something below. "This always happens!" Earl said. "Sorry, Grandpa, I'm going to have to break the line."

The small boat rocked alarmingly as both boys leaned far over the gunwale, trying to see where the line was caught. *At that very moment, Ed saw it!* Peeking out from a rotten piece of planking was the perfectly round top of a bottle! He had only a split second's view of it until Earl's thrashing about moved their boat a little and the thing was out of sight.

Ed was making plans so fast he hardly heard the conversation from the others. He meant to retrieve that bottle, if that's what it was, and he planned to tell no one about it. He'd have to get rid of Earl that was sure. He nearly overlooked the necessity of taking a "sight" on something ashore. He'd need to know about where the wreck lay when he was back on the beach. The same black rock Earl had showed him was perfect. He kept it in view as long as possible.

"Go ahead and break the line, Earl. I've got lots more tackle. You want to catch some?" he asked Ed.

"Nope. I'm not much of a fisherman, and as I said, we were always too busy on the farm in summers. Thanks anyway."

They pulled up the anchor and headed back. The breeze had freshened some, so they only had to row a little. The wind was pushing them right back!

"You o.k.? Not seasick are you?" Frank asked as they neared their landing place.

"No, not at all, but you should have seen me a week ago Sunday when I came over for the day cruise. Never been so sick in my life!"

"I was in the navy, so I know what you mean. The old joke was that at first you were scared that a German sub was going to torpedo you r ship, but when you got seasick enough you were hoping one would!" Frank grinned, but Ed noticed a sort of distant look in the old man's eyes.

Ed told them about his brother being a frogman in World War

Two, but Frank just nodded, saying nothing. Evidently he had said all he was going to about the war.

"Come on in, my boy. Carrie's the best fish fryer on the island. We'll show you what fish right out of the lake really taste like."

"No thanks," Ed replied. "I need to do some more work at my camp. It was nice of you to treat me to breakfast though, and thanks for the boat ride."

"I'll come with you," Earl exclaimed.

"No Earl. You come on in and eat now. Then you're to lie down for an hour. You mom's coming over the fourth of July and we want her to find you healthy."

"But Grandpa . . "

"No." Frank didn't raise his voice. He didn't need to.

The next morning Ed was up early. His snorkeling gear laid out and ready, but it was too rough to think about trying to swim out to the wreck site. He pottered around the camp, cooked some pancakes for breakfast, and washed his few dishes in the lake. He was expecting to see Earl come running down the beach, but the boy never showed up. Ed was pretty sure Earl's grandparents had kept him home, afraid the boy was making a nuisance of himself. He was glad, but had to admit he sort of enjoyed the younger boy's company. Also he felt a little sorry for him. It appeared that by age fifteen, he'd had a pretty tough time of it. He got Eli's diary out of the cookie can and re-read quite a bit of it. Of course "diary number one" had no mention of old Eli's later adventures on Beaver Island. All of that was in diary number two.

With nothing better to do, he climbed into his car and turned on the radio. In less than five minutes he had fallen fast asleep. When he awoke he quickly started the engine, afraid he might have run the battery down. "Well," he said aloud, "as long as the motor's running I think I'll go up to the village. Maybe get a bottle of pop."

Not much was happening in the small town. He struck up a conversation with a fisherman who was at work on his nets down near the ferry dock. The "conversation" was mostly one-sided, as the old man only nodded occasionally or grunted a sort of reply, his pipe never leaving his mouth.

Just as he was heading for his car it dawned on him. "Boy am I dumb!" he thought, pulling out of the parking lot. "I should be getting ready to get out to the wreck site the minute the weather breaks!" He assumed that Frank was not about to let him borrow the boat, so more urgent matters were called for.

CHAPTER FOURTEEN

Treasure!

He had neither ax nor saw, so the raft he was intending to build would be no thing of beauty. There was plenty of driftwood all up and down the beach, but most of it was too small for much buoyancy. Pulling on his jacket in an attempt to fool the mosquitoes, he plunged into the deep forest, searching for logs. They would have to be free of rot and light enough for him to drag them to the beach. Finding three that would serve, although far from ideal, he slid them along, sweating and panting. Rolling them to the very edge of the water, he began lashing them together with his new rope. He left one end hang free and tied on a large rock for his anchor.

He sliced up a potato for this supper, listened to the radio for a while, then crawled into bed.

Awake before dawn, he listened for the sound of the waves. Unable to hear a thing, he dressed quickly and ran down to the shore. It was flat calm! How he wished he had a hammer and a few nails. "I could have a driftwood deck on this monstrosity in no time," he thought. He waded out until the water was up to his knees. It was like walking barefoot in snow. He'd had no idea how cold Michigan water could be this early in summer!

He paid no attention to the beautiful sunrise out over Lake Michigan. He wanted to get out to the wreck before Earl showed up, asking a million questions. He eased his body forward, trying to lie across his unwieldy raft. The logs shifted as he tried to paddle, the cold was agonizing, and his stone "anchor" slipped off and plunged to the bottom! "This ain't going to work!" Ed told himself, his teeth chattering so hard no one else could have understood a word. "O.k., You old beast. Stay anchored right there. I'm going back to the shore! Why am I talking to myself?" he wondered.

Running to the tent, he stripped off his dripping overalls and underwear, and wrapped up in a blanket. When he finally stopped shivering he dressed in dry clothes and hung the wet ones on his clothesline. The thin cord, stretched between two trees behind his tent gave him an idea. He threw the soaked things over some bushes and untied his clothesline.

He ran up and down the beach just to get warmed up, but as he did so he gathered driftwood into a pile at the wreck site. The dry wood caught quickly, only one match being needed. When it was burning well he ran back to his car. Grinning to himself he dug into the clutter in the back seat until he found what he was looking for. "Never thought I'd need these, Mom," he thought, pulling out the "long Johns" she had insisted he take to Michigan. Another inspiration came. With Tom's sleeping bag and the long johns under one arm, he grabbed the snorkeling equipment and sprinted back to the fire.

Pulling the ugly red garment on, he found himself constantly looking back over his shoulder. He figured Earl would be coming pretty soon. Ed liked the boy well enough, but he had no intention of sharing the treasure with him or anybody else!

The face mask fit perfectly, but as he had learned earlier, the swim fins were too large. He filled the toes with rolled up socks, adjusted the snorkel, took a deep breath, and started swimming. Getting the anchor back on the raft was a struggle but he managed it. Thankful that there was hardly any wind, he paddled toward the wreck site. Luck was with him. He came across the *Caroline's* remains on his first try. The sun was completely up by this time, and even half frozen as he was, he marveled at the clarity of the water. He pushed the anchor rock off the logs, filled his lungs, and dived.

He made it all the way to the jumbled rocks and rotten boards on the bottom. He could not find the top of the bottle he'd seen from Mr. Coleson's boat the day before. He surfaced, gasping for breath. Too much oxygen and energy was consumed just by swimming down to the wreck. "One more try!" he told himself. He was so cold he could hardly think straight. Back at the raft he grabbed the anchor rope and pulled himself down hand over hand, which allowed him another half minute or so on the bottom.

There! The small round top of the bottle was in plain sight, only partly covered by an ancient piece of timber. Ed grabbed it. Thankfully it came free easily. Holding the slippery bottle, he started for the surface, but as he rose he suddenly saw what appeared to be two more bottles lying on their sides under the same board as the one he'd moved. There was no time to investigate further! Ears ringing, he burst into the air, gasping and choking. He was scared. Very scared! "You idiot," he thought, "you could drown yourself. No more staying down that long!" He was shaking, but not only from the cold!

Clutching the object to his chest, one arm and his fins propelled into the shallow water. The raft remained anchored over the wreck as he hurried to the fire. Stripping the soggy long johns, he crawled into Tom's sleeping bag, only realizing that he should have laid it on the sand. Rocks jabbed him in many places but he didn't care. It was *warm* in the big cocoon! Ed was aware that he was spending a lot of time and energy just to retrieve an old bottle, but when he got back home it would be proof that he had found the treasure ship.

Warming up at last, he pulled on dry jeans and a sweatshirt he had thought to leave by the fire. He squatted as close to the flames as possible and picked up the bottle. It was identical to the broken one Earl had found some time before. Carefully he rubbed off the slippery junk that had accumulated over the past one hundred and twenty years. The base was square, the thin neck attached by a graceful fluted section of brown glass. Words began to appear. Raised letters were quite distinct: **BORDAINE-LEVEQUE FINE WHISKEY MONTREAL.**

Soaking up heat from the fire, Ed was suddenly struck by a horrible thought. Eli's diary had often mentioned boss Avery whispering to his henchmen about getting "cases". "That's it," the boy thought glumly. "There never was any treasure aboard the *Caroline*. It wasn't gold bars or silver coins at all. *It was whiskey!* Just old cases of booze!"

He wanted to cry, or scream, or curse. "All of my plans and all of my work just for a few old bottles, for Pete's sake!" He drew back his arm, ready to throw the little bottle back into the lake, when he heard a car horn honking. "That will be Earl, I'm sure," he thought as he stuffed the bottle deep into Tom's sleeping bag.

"Hey Ed, look what I've got." Earl came striding along the beach holding up a package. "Marshmallows," he shouted, "and you've already got a fire going...wow! Have you been swimming? The water must be like ice in the lake. Why don't you go to one of the little lakes here on the island? The water's always way warmer in them. I'll get some sticks to roast these on."

Ed had to grin as the boy hurried off to get some green branches. His friend may have had some serious problems, but it certainly didn't keep him from talking!

They sat by the fire and burned their fingers on the blackened treats. "Is that a raft out there? Is this your snorkeling equipment? How'd you get that raft out there? You don't have a boat do you?"

"Slow down Earl. *Slow down!* Yes, it's a raft, or at least the best one I could make with no tools. As for the snorkeling stuff, they actually belong to my dad. He's going to give them to my older brother when he gets back from Lebanon."

"Hey Earl, do you want some lunch? I'm about starved. You're right about Lake Michigan water. It is cold man, cold!"

"Did you get the raft clear out to the wreck? See any fish? Sure, I'm hungry too. Are you going to cook?"

"I don't see anybody else around here, do you?" Ed laughed. "Say, you want to do something for me? Run over to the cook stove back of the tent and bring me the big kettle. I'll need to douse this fire."

"Sure Ed, I'll get it, but I'm not supposed to run. That asthma I got, see?"

"Oh, I forgot about that. Sorry. Just take your time. I need to straighten up here anyway." As soon as Earl had gone he hid the bottle in a hollow stump at the edge of the forest.

X   X   X

Thank heaven for Earl's "nap time", Ed was thinking as the Ford bounced and jostled its way over the unpaved road to the village. He had seen a sort of run-down looking antique shop there on his first visit. He was planning to try to sell the bottle, thinking he might get enough out of it to pay his passage back to the mainland. It was Saturday and he wanted to leave on the Sunday afternoon boat. His days on the island had seemed to fly past, but in that short time he had learned to love the place. "I'm coming back here on my honeymoon!" he told himself with a chuckle.

He pressed the doorbell as the little sign said. No one came so he rang the bell again.

"I'm *coming!*" A raspy voice yelled. The door hinges grated and a rather unkempt woman stood there staring at him. "What do you want?" she growled, still not inviting him in.

"I've got something to sell if you're interested."

"What is it?"

"It's an old square bottle. I think it may be over a hundred years old."

"You got it with you?"

"Sure. It's in the car. I'll get it."

Reluctantly, it seemed, she let him in. There were several glass front cases and many long shelves. Old pictures hung on every wall.

"Where'd you get this, kid?" she croaked.

"Well I've been camping down on the south end of the island, and . . ."

"Lemme see that. Just an old bottle. Don't look like no hundred years old to me, and I'm in the business."

"O.k., sure. Sorry to bother you." He reached out for the bottle she was still holding. He sort of wanted to take it back to Ohio anyway.

"Just a minute. I'll be right back." Very carefully she set the whiskey bottle on the counter and went into another room. Before she jerked the curtain closed behind her, Ed could see shelves of new-looking books and catalogues. It was perhaps ten minutes until she returned. "I kind of like the looks of that old bottle you found. Tell you what. I'll give you two dollars for it."

Ed's dad had taught him how to deal when getting a price for hay or wheat seed at the grain elevator. Like most boys his age, he had also argued with the occasional used car salesman. He pretended to ponder her offer for a moment, then shook his head. "I guess I'll just keep it for a souvenir," he said. He reached for the bottle.

"Wait a minute! I told you it's not that old. My offer is fair, but I guess I can go three dollars."

"Thanks, but the more I think about it," Ed murmured, "the more I'd like to have it on my dresser at home."

"*Four dollars!* And it ain't worth half that. I'm a fool to even offer you that kind of money for an old bottle."

"Gee, that's very nice of you," Ed said politely, "but you know, I guess I'll keep it though."

"Well *keep it then!*" she snorted, slamming the door behind him.

Cradling the bottle in both hands, Ed half ran to his car. "Thanks Dad!" he said aloud. Dollar signs were starting to appear in his mind. "That old woman was trying to beat me out of a good deal, but it was just like Dad always said, 'if they're willing to keep on raising the price they'll pay, then they know something you don't.'"

Bumping along the rough road to his camp, he was getting more and more excited. It was obvious that the antique dealer had managed to find the true value of that whiskey bottle in one of her catalogues. If she was willing to pay four dollars for it, it had to be worth at least twice that much so she could resell it for a profit. He was thinking so fast he nearly missed a sharp curve in the road. "Let's see, eight bucks,

well say seven bucks each! I've got one bottle right here and I'm pretty sure I can get those other two I saw down on the wreck. Twenty one *bucks!* I'd have had to pick cherries over *four full days* to make that much. I can't wait to tell Mom and Dad. And *Junior!*"

Before he even reached his camp site he saw a small figure sitting on a rock near the shore. He was not surprised. He felt sorry for Earl, but still he wrapped the bottle in his jacket before he got out of the car.

"Hi Ed. Where you been? I've been waiting for you for about an hour. Have you had any dinner? We ate already but Grandma could find you something if you haven't eaten yet. Were you in town?"

"Easy, Earl, easy. Yeah, I was in town for a while. Had some business to attend to. I'm going to fry up some potatoes for my lunch. Come on over to the kitchen. You mind starting the kerosene stove while I peel the potatoes?"

"Sure Ed. I know how to do it since you showed me. What business was it in town?"

"Just business. So your mom's coming on the fourth?" he said, quickly changing the subject.

"She *says* she's coming, but sometimes she changes her mind about stuff. She's kinda messed up. I guess the divorce caused it. I sure hope she does come though. Grandpa and Grandma are pretty nice most of the time, but well, you know, they're really old and everything."

"Ever see you dad at all?"

"Yeah, a couple times last winter. We went to a restaurant. He took me to a movie once. I think we were both glad when his visits were over. He's o.k., but he drinks a lot. He won't be coming up here though. I guess he don't want to see Grandma and Grandpa."

"I'm sorry for you, but I can see you're a pretty tough guy. You'll handle it."

"Me tough? Not hardly! Are you really gonna leave tomorrow?" Earl asked, fiddling with the stove. "I wish you could stay a while. We could do lots of stuff together. You could meet my mom and . . ."

"I have to Earl. I'd like to stay longer too, but I've been gone too long already."

"What do you mean 'too long'?"

"I live on a farm. Dad's going to need lots of help for the rest of the summer and fall. Like right now, the wheat's probably just about ready to come off, then there's hay to put up, corn to pick, on and on it goes."

"That must be great! Earl breathed. "Living on a farm and everything. Bet your dad's fun to be around. Like you are."

"Look at this," Ed said, pulling a lock of hair off his forehead. "See that scar? That's how much *fun* my dad can be sometimes."

"Your dad hit you?" Earl was incredulous. "My dad never hit me, even when he was drunk. What did you do that made him hit you?"

"Lots of things, but the worst was that me and a couple buddies stole a barrel of hard cider. We got caught."

"Wow!" Earl's admiration knew no bounds! "You sure you have to leave tomorrow? You could stay at our house. Grandma and Grandpa wouldn't mind. You could have my bed. I'd sleep on the sofa. No mosquitoes or anything. How about it?"

"Sorry Earl. Thanks for asking though. Have you had your nap yet today? You better not miss it, since your mom's coming and everything."

The boy looked very sad, but Ed had one more dive to make and it wouldn't do to have Earl watching everything. "Tell you what," Ed said, finishing the last of the fried potatoes, "why don't you go home, have your nap, and I'll drive up in a couple hours and we can take a ride all around in my car. Did you ever do any driving at all?"

Earl's face lit up like a beacon. "You got it! That would be super. But listen, I only sleep for a little while. Why don't you come a lot sooner than you said?"

"I got things to do Earl. I'll be at your house in a little over two hours, o.k.?"

"Well I guess, but come as soon as you can." He hurried away down the beach, careful not to run.

Ed sprang into action the minute Earl was out of sight. While driving back to his camp he'd had an idea. There had to be an easier way to retrieve the two remaining bottles. They might be stuck down there, and he didn't relish the thought of trying to pull them free while his breath was nearly gone. He folded up the dry clothes from the line and threw them into the tent. Next he untied the thin cord and fashioned a small slipknot on one end. Finding a smooth stick about five feet long, he tied the noose near the end of it. "By golly, I think maybe I can *lasso* those babies!" he thought.

He threw new driftwood in the fire ring he'd used before and lighted a fire. When it was burning well he ran to the tent for his snorkeling equipment. Stripped to his underwear, he pulled the now dry long johns on, waded out a ways, and swam to the raft. The water was every bit as cold as before, but he tried to ignore its bite.

Unfortunately the lake was no longer calm, and the raft had drifted several yards. It was a struggle to propel the unwieldy logs through the waves, even with the considerable help of his swim fins. He had trouble locating the wreck, as wave action lifted him, then lowered his body a foot or so every few seconds. At last he saw the familiar pile of rubble below. The raft anchored, he slipped off the logs and pulled himself down, the stick with the noose aimed like a spear at the bottom.

Luck [or something else] was certainly with him. He saw the tops of the two bottles clearly enough, but he was too far away for an attempt to snag one of them. He surfaced, breathed deeply, and dived again. This time he was right on target. The extra reach provided by the stick was just what was needed. The slipknot settled just below the hand-blown bulb on the neck. Gently, his breath running out, he drew the line tight. Surfacing with the stick firmly in hand he began to pull.

There was tension at first, but suddenly the bottle came free, raising a cloud of silt. Ed took no chances. He swam until he could touch bottom, waded onto the shore, and secured the bottle under a piece of driftwood. *Success!*

The second bottle was more difficult. By the time he had finally fished it out he was dangerously numb and cold. Placing it carefully beside its companion he stripped to his shorts and huddled over the fire. As soon as he was thawed enough to stop shivering somewhat, he ran to his tent and climbed into some dry clothes. He wrapped the bottles separately in various items of clothing and secured them on the back seat under Tom's still wet sleeping bag.

"Hey Ed!" It was Earl, picking his way through the stones along the beach. "I got awake from my nap so they said I could come on over. What you been doing?"

"*Just got done in time!*" Ed breathed in relief as the boy hurried up.

"You been swimming again? Your hair's all wet."

"Yep. One last dip. Water was really cold too!"

"Like I said, you could have gone to one of the inland lakes. The water's always a lot warmer in them. I can't go swimming yet, but Grandma said I could go when the weather gets hot. Probably August she says. Did you go out to the wreck on your raft? Why don't you tie a couple more logs on it? You could almost stay dry that way. What do you think?"

Ed couldn't help laughing, but he knew the boy was really starved for someone to talk to. "That's a good idea Earl. Should have thought of it myself, but it's too late now. My rafting days are over. Want to help me roll the logs back off the beach?" He was careful to do the bulk of the work himself, while allowing his friend to think he was doing some pushing too.

"Grandpa and Grandma want you to come over for supper. Why don't you come right now? They want to talk to you some before you have to leave tomorrow. You still panning to go then, are you?"

"Sure." Ed replied coiling the half inch rope over his arm. "How about helping me put some of this stuff in the car? You want to take a ride around the island? I'll let you drive some of the time."

"That would be *great!* Where should I put these clothes? What the heck is *this?*" Earl asked. He was holding the long stick with the clothesline still attached.

"Oh that? I was trying to see if I could pull up anything off the wreck. Pretty silly-looking isn't it?"

"Did it work? Did you get anything with it?"

"You do know how to drive, don't you?" Ed asked hurriedly. He didn't like the way the conversation was heading.

"Yeah, I know how. Grandpa's been showing me but he never lets me go very far. Just up and down the beach road, and he says twenty miles an hour is fast enough for anybody!"

Relieved, Ed laughed a little. "Well he's right about that. These roads are so rough, going much faster would about shake a car to pieces. Hop in Pal. Let's do some driving before we go to your place."

"I don't know Ed. Maybe they wouldn't want me to drive your car, and also .. ."

"I have some good advice for you, Earl. Treat your Grandparents right, but don't tell them everything! I'll drive till we're past the cottage."

X   X   X

Carrie Coleson poured a second cup of cocoa and handed the boys a plate of cookies. "So that's how you keep the old diary safe? In that cookie can?"

"Yep. Mom would skin me alive if anything happened to the originals. They were handed down to her from way back in her family."

"Did you say 'originals'?" Frank asked. "Were there more than one?"

"Yes, there are two of them. This is the first one. I've finished translating both of them now. I send my translations to my brother, who's a diver for DEEP WATER ENTERPRISES over in Lebanon Do you want to see what I do with them?" he handed Mr. Coleson his notebook.

"The old fellow was certainly no speller, was he?" Frank laughed, handing Ed's notebook to his wife. "But why are you writing everything exactly as the old man wrote it?"

"I do it that way because Junior, that's my brother, gets a kick out of seeing them like they really were written. We don't dare risk sending the originals. Mom says he and his wife need stuff to cheer them up over there in Lebanon. So we send a package over whenever I get a batch finished."

"Ed, I don't mean to pry, but I'm guessing that these diaries have told you something about our island, and about the *Caroline.* Is that it?" Frank was obviously a very perceptive individual!

Ed hesitated for only a moment. These people had been good to him, and any fool could see they were a trustworthy couple. Also, he just couldn't wait any longer to tell *somebody* the story.

"I'll leave the translations with you tonight, but don't let me forget to get them before I leave tomorrow. You can read some of it if you want to. You have to be a little creative, but it gets easier as you get into it."

"I can see why you call all your work a 'translation'," Frank said, shaking his head, "we'll enjoy this."

"I didn't bring the second diary with me. I was lucky that Mom finally agreed to let me take this one. I happened to read his second diary first. In that one he tells about taking a load of logs to Chicago. They landed here on Beaver Island, but after they left the harbor the *Caroline* sank."

"But everyone on the island says there were no survivors," Frank said.

"Actually, according to the diary, there were two. Eli, He's the writer, missed the boat when it left the island. His best friend, a young man named Billy, was injured when the *Caroline's* boiler exploded. He made it to shore but died soon after. I think maybe his grave is located in a cemetery back of the church."

"I've seen that boiler," Frank said. "On my first trip out here years ago it was lying in shallow water right beside the wreck. Later on, the islanders said it was hauled away during the war and sold for scrap."

Earl had said little during the conversation, but he'd missed not a word. "Do you think we could find that old guy's grave? Must be a tombstone or something with his name on it."

"I doubt it," Ed replied. "Probably wouldn't be anything showing after a hundred and twenty years. May not even have been a tombstone or anything either. Just keep your eyes peeled for Billy's ghost!"

"How about the *Captain's* ghost?" Carrie laughed.

Frank squinted his eyes and proclaimed, "I saw the Captain just last week. He was sort of floating, right outside the loft window above Earl's bed! AWWOOO!"

"Frank! For heaven's sake. Do you want to frighten your grandson to death?"

"Aw it's o.k., Grandma. I'm not afraid of ghosts anymore, Captains or not."

As they ate supper it began to rain, and the wind was rising as well.

"Oh boy!" Ed growled. "This is going to mean packing up a wet tent again! Well, I can handle it. Maybe it'll be sunny tomorrow. I can load it up then."

It was nearly dark by the time Ed told them he had to get back to camp. They begged him to spend the night at the cottage but he was getting anxious about the rising wind. "I'll have to go and make sure my tent isn't heading for Chicago!"

"I can come and help," Earl said miserably, glancing at his grandparents.

"I know you'd help me out if you could, but you can hear that wind and rain. Tell you what. After your nap tomorrow if it's not raining come on over to my camp. I could use some help then. That is if you want to."

"Sure I want to," Earl said. "I don't sleep very long anymore so I'll be coming over there pretty soon after we have our breakfast.

CHAPTER 15

Heading Home to Face the Music

The tent was in a shambles. The pegs had pulled loose in the wind, even though he'd piled heavy rocks on each one. Puddles of water lay all over the canvas. Luckily the tent had collapsed almost on top of the door opening, so his cot and blankets had not been soaked. There was nothing he could do as the wind and rain persisted.

"I should have got back here the minute the rain started," he chided himself. "Well there's always the front seat of the Ford."

He spent another miserable night with hardly any sleep. The rain continued off and on, and the wind was so strong he could hear the loose tent flapping with every gust.

Morning finally arrived. It was no longer raining, but the clouds were low and threatening to unload again. In a foul mood, it did not occur to the boy to think what his time on Beaver Island would have been if he'd had this kind of weather at the beginning of his week.

Stiff and sore from trying to sleep in the car, he knew he'd better get at it. For a few more minutes he sat glowering out of the windshield, watching the wind whip the branches of the nearby cedars. It was cold in the car but he didn't start the engine. Even if the heater worked, idling while the engine warmed up would waste gas, which cost *twenty six cents a gallon!* Naturally his coat and cap were somewhere under the collapsed tent, probably soaking wet. "Well," he mumbled aloud, "if I can make six or seven dives in water that cold, a little rain won't be so bad."

It was full daylight now, but the sun was hidden behind banks of low-lying clouds, driven ever eastward by the strongest wind he'd yet experienced. The waves crashed against the shore in a lather of foam with almost hypnotic regularity.

Leaving the car door hanging open, he ran to the tent, found the door flap, and managed to almost burrow his way inside. His cot was still standing, although the stays had collapsed on one end. Ed wrestled it around until it propped up one side of the tent. Working mostly by feel, he he pulled out various items, dashed to the car and threw them into the back seat. Fortunately most of his gear was still dry, but he was soaked to the skin.

"How in the world will I ever get this tent folded up in this wind?" he thought. At that moment the rain began again.

Sitting in the car once more, his wet jeans soaking the driver's seat, he suddenly became aware of headlights jouncing over the rocks toward him.

It was Frank and Earl!

"You better stay in the car," Frank said as Earl was preparing to get out. "Let's get this wet chicken back to the cottage for some hot coffee and a big breakfast!"

"I'll get your car seats all wet," Ed protested, but Frank paid no attention. In no time they were back at the cottage. Fire in the stove, coffee brewing in the kitchen, and a hot shower waiting. Heaven itself could not have felt better!

After an early lunch they were glad to see the sun finally appear, although the wind seemed as strong as ever. With Frank's help they were able to fold the dripping tent and pack it down in the back seat. Both were wet by the time the job was done, but Grandpa didn't seem to mind.

"I don't know how to thank you." Ed had driven his loaded car to the cottage and they were drying off with towels Carrie handed them.

"That's a neat lamp," Ed said, eyeing a tall nickel-plated oil lamp on the table.

"I love it. It belonged to my grandmother. I hardly ever light it but after a night like we just had it's sort of a comfort, don't you think?" Ms. Coleson was smiling as the lamplight reflected off her glasses. "I like antiques. There's a little shop right here on the island, but Miss Graves is kind of hard to deal with. I showed her my lamp and she wanted to buy it."

"*Steal it,* you mean!" Frank growled.

"To tell the truth I had no intention of selling it anyway. I was just curious to see what it might be worth. If I ever did decide to sell any of my antiques I'd take them to <u>MY TREASURES.</u> It's a very nice antique shop in Charlevoix."

Ed had never listened to anything more closely! "What time is it now?" he asked.

"One fifteen," Earl answered. "Did you get everything closed up o.k.? Was you tent ruined? Wish I could have helped. I would have if it hadn't rained so much and all that wind. Did you get wet sleeping? How was . . ."

"Slow down, Earl. You hardly give Ed a chance to get a word in," Mrs. Coleson chided.

"It's o.k. Mrs. Coleson, Earl's been a good helper and a real friend. What say we write to each other, Earl?"

"That would be *great!* Let's do that."

"Mr. Coleson, isn't there a two o'clock boat from the island on Sundays?"

Frank consulted a brochure he took from a drawer. "Yes, there is. Are you planning to leave on that run?"

"Well I hadn't really decided, but if I can make it in time I could be clear back home by maybe seven or eight tonight. Just in time to do my chores!" he laughed.

X   X   X

The loading ramp was shifting alarmingly as Ed eased his car aboard. "Pull up close to that Studebaker," the attendant said. "Set your parking brake and put her in first gear. It's gonna be one rough crossing! The Coast Guard says this has to be our last crossing today. They wouldn't even allow this run if it wasn't for the 'day people' needing to get back. Hang onto your hat!"

Ed went on deck for less than five minutes, just to see the waves smashing into *Star Shine's* stubby bows. Every few minutes he could feel the railings shift with the erratic movement of the boat. Alarming bumps and clanking noises did nothing to reassure him. Feeling queasy already, he hurried down to the lower deck and climbed into his car. The smell of wet canvas, spoiled food, and an open jar of peanut butter did not help!

Like before, he was sick during the whole voyage. Twice he had to hurry up to the small salon to use the rest room. Someone had been there before and had vomited all over the place, but that did not make him any sicker than he was. Nothing could!

Even in the sheltered harbor at Charlevoix, the *Star Shine* continued to pitch and roll. With much difficulty and clanging of bells, she finally was able to back into the off-loading berth.

The seven cars eased their way onto the dock, Ed's Ford among them. The moment he was on the street he pulled off into a parking space, yanked the door open, and lost what little remained in his stomach.

"Got just what you need mister."

"Who are you?" Ed growled, wiping his face with his handkerchief.

"I run that stand over there," the old man answered, jerking his head to the left. "I knew there would be folks upchucking like crazy the minute the car ferry got secured. Like I said, I've got just what you need!"

"What is it?" Ed mumbled.

"Come on over. It's ginger ale. It'll fix you right up. Look at them already over there. They're taking my advice. You ought to do the same."

Ed stared bleary-eyed at four people leaning against the little stand, gulping at bottles of ginger ale as fast as they could. He bought two bottles, drank them fast, and handed the empties back. It was almost a miracle! He began feeling better right away. He didn't notice the proprietor grinning to himself. He'd found a way to boost his sales, selling his product before the seasick travelers realized that being on solid ground, they would very soon feel better anyway! "Oh well," he justified his actions, "it's only a nickel a bottle."

Recovering rapidly, Ed approached the man again. "Say mister, do you know where the antique store called MY TREASURES is located?"

"Why sure. Take this street down to Birch Avenue and make a left. It's on the next corner."

Ed stopped at a small gas station on the way. While the attendant was filling the tank he used the restroom to try to clean himself up a little. There wasn't anything he could do about the stains on his shirt.

"Hey kid, you got a problem here. Take a look."

He held the dipstick up for Ed to see. The oil was barely touching the bottom. "You better get some more oil in this buggy before you go another mile. You don't, you're risking a ruined engine!"

"O.k. One quart. And would you mind putting some air in that left rear tire? Looks a little low."

The man dumped in the single quart of oil, pumped up the tire, took Ed's money, and stomped away. It had not been the kind of sale he was hoping for.

Two other cars were parked in front of MY TREASURES. Both were much newer and more expensive than Ed's ford. He went in, one of the whiskey bottles wrapped up in a damp towel. The owner, plump and pretty, was showing a customer a small brass figurine. She smiled at Ed, but continued with the well-dressed lady.

As Ed stood waiting, he noticed that another couple kept moving away from him. He wondered why. Then it struck him. He *stank!* Wet canvas, old tennis shoes, recent vomit, take your pick. Any or all of them could be the culprit. Embarrassed, he moved back to one corner of the shop, as far from anyone as possible. All the other customers left, rather hurriedly it seemed!

"How can I help you, young man?"

"Ma'am, I'm afraid I don't smell very good. I just got off the ferry from Beaver Island. Just about everyone on it was seasick, me worst of all. I'm on my way home to Ohio, and haven't had a chance to clean up. Sorry!"

"Come right on up here. I've had hay fever all my life. That's why I moved up here from Cleveland. To tell you the truth I can't smell a thing. Haven't been able to for years. Now what are you interested in?"

With a sigh of relief, Ed unwrapped the whiskey bottle. "I thought you might want to buy this old bottle."

"Let me see that." She held it up to the window and peered at it for a long time. "What's inside of it?" she asked, giving him a very careful appraisal.

"I don't know. Maybe just sand and stuff. I think I could clean that out of there if you're interested. And if you 've got some steel wool I'll clean those stains off the outside too."

"*Never!*" she almost gasped. "Never clean up an antique unless you're an expert! Where did you get this?"

"Found it in the water over on the island. Is it worth anything at all?"

A very strange smile lit up her dimpled cheeks. "Well let's see if it is," she said mysteriously.

A set of catalogues which appeared to be much like the ones he'd caught a glimpse of at the Beaver Island antique shop lined several shelves behind the counter. It didn't take her but a few minutes. "Yes, they are worth something. They list at one thirty-five, but I can't pay that much. I have to make a profit you know. I'll give you eighty-five for it. What do you say?"

Ed felt a little sick. He could have been paid four dollars for the bottle over on the island. "I've got another one just like it. Would you be interested?"

"Of course! Let's see it."

Another couple was entering the shop as Ed headed out to his car. Coming back with the second bottle, he noticed the newcomers seemed to linger on the far side of the room! He handed the small bottle to the lady. She took much longer examining this one.

"There's a good-sized chip broken from the foot here." She pointed it out to him. "I can only go seventy for this one."

"Serves you right, smart guy!" Ed told himself silently. "But still that makes a dollar fifty-five total. That will buy me a little over five gallons of gas. Better than nothing, I guess."

"O.k., I'll take it," he told her.

"Fine! Would you like cash or a check?"

Ed laughed a little. The lady couldn't miss making fun of his "big purchase"! "I'll take cash I guess," he mumbled.

"I'll just be a minute," she said, placing the bottles very carefully in a glass front cabinet almost identical to the one in which his mother had kept Eli's diaries. She locked the cabinet and disappeared through a side door.

Ed stood on one foot, then the other. This was taking a lot longer than he'd thought. He wished he'd sold the bottles on the island, but there was nothing he could do about it now. He just wanted to get started for Ohio.

"I wish to thank you for allowing me the opportunity of buying these very fine antique bottles." She opened a fancy leather wallet, took out a sheaf of ten dollar bills and began counting them out. "Eighty-five plus seventy equals one hundred fifty-five dollars. I'll put it in an envelope for you."

Ed was so astonished that he was halfway out the door before he turned and thanked her effusively.

"If you ever come across any more of these rare Canadian whiskeys I'd like first chance to buy them from you. Bottle collectors love them, as that company was only in business for a few years."

Ed was not even tempted to sell his one remaining bottle, sure now that he could always sell it later. "You can be sure of that! Thank you! Thank you! *Thank you!*" He leaped into his car and scattered gravel on his way out of the parking lot. He pointed the Ford south and let out a big *yippee!*

Eli's ungrammatical diaries had led him to a treasure all right. Not gold or silver, but bottles! Antique Canadian whiskey bottles turned out to be the true treasure of Beaver Island. But there was still another treasure waiting!

X   X   X

Just outside of town he found a larger service station. He had a young attendant add two quarts of oil. As the boy was cleaning the windshield, Ed had an inspiration. "Do you sell oil by the case?" he asked.

"Nope. No discount for a case. You have to pay the price per quart no matter how many you get. We're a small station. Can't afford to do what some of the big boys do. It'll cost you three eighty-four for twelve cans. Sorry."

"That's o.k. I'll take twelve cans. Here's the money for the oil and four chocolate bars. Keep fifty cents for yourself!"

"Hey, thanks buddy! Say, you got a girlfriend? I see you have an Ohio license plate. Better take your sweetie a present."

Inside, Ed looked over a table of cheap knickknacks meant for the tourists who were starting to arrive in the area. For his mom he selected a small seagull pin, and for his dad a nail clipper with the word "Charlevoix" printed on it. He was sure his dad would never use it, but it was something to give him.

Back in his car he sat a minute, slightly stunned. In the past hour he'd made more money and *spent* more money than he had in his whole life!

Chomping on a candy bar, he was finally headed home.

X   X   X

It was almost nine o'clock when he finally pulled slowly into his driveway. The pole light was on. His mother came rushing out to greet him, but there was no sign of his dad. Ed knew that a confrontation was inevitable, and that it might get physical. He was too tired to care.

"Eddie, *Eddie* we were so *worried!* Where have you *been?*"

"Why Momma, I've been picking. You know that."

Cal appeared from the living room, newspaper in hand. "Not *all this time* you weren't!"

"But Dad, I . . ."

"Don't lie to me, boy. I know what you've been up to. Or most of it anyway. When your mother got so worried I called Tom's father. They made him tell what you were planning to do up there."

"I didn't do anything wrong, Dad. I just wanted to . . ."

"*Shut up!* When I want to hear from you I'll say so. Up on that stupid island, running around 'looking for treasure'." He said the last three words in a disgusting falsetto voice.

"Your work up there was all done more than a week ago. I've been doing your chores *and mine* for longer than I needed to."

"But Dad. . . Mom . . . I actually found . . ."

"*Shut up* I said!" he advanced on his son, his arm raised to strike.

"Cal, stop it! Eddie just got home, and . . ."

"*Go ahead!*" Ed shouted. "Smack me around a little, but I'm telling you this is the *last time.* I'll be seventeen in two months. I was on my own for a month, and I've come home with more money than you'll make all summer. I'm tired, I'm hungry, and I smell like puke. You hit me once more, and you'd better be ready for a fight!"

"Eddie, you father didn't mean it. We were just so worried when we found out you had left the orchards. We're just glad you're home at last."

"Well," Eddie said, facing his father once more, "maybe he didn't mean it, but *I did!*"

There was total silence for a full minute. All three stood as if rooted in place. Then, of all the surprises and unexpected things that had happened to him over the last month, the most amazing event took place right there in the dining room. "Good enough, Ed. Looks like you've done a lot of growing up these past weeks. You go on up and get a shower. I'll look for you at chore time tomorrow."

Ed was close to tears as he saw just the faintest flicker of something almost like approval on his father's face. Up in his room after a shower he stretched out on his bed. His mother brought a plate of food, but he was already asleep. She left, smiling.

Chores went fine after the biggest breakfast he'd had since the Coleson's cottage on Beaver Island. Old Curly turned a suspicious cow's eye on him, not having seen him for a while, but she didn't kick this time. After the cream separator was emptied and sterilized Ed and his mother sat down at the kitchen table. "I want to hear all about your trip," Beth said, filling two coffee cups. "Don't leave out a single thing!"

The kitchen door opened, and Cal pulled a chair up to the table, took Beth's coffee cup, and settled himself. "Me too," he remarked. "Mainly I'd like to know how you got more money than I can make on this farm. You sure as heck never made much picking fruit." He was still the same father, but both Ed and his mother could detect something somehow a little different about the man.

"Wait right here," Ed shouted, sprinting to his car. There was a moment of panic when he couldn't put his hands on the envelope from the antique shop, but he finally found it on the back seat under the wet tent. Without removing the shirt he'd wrapped it in, he took the bottle and hurried back to the kitchen. Feeling like a carnival magician, he spread the bills out on the red oil cloth.

"Where'd you get all that money son?" Cal was suddenly sounding much like his old self again, suspicious and cynical.

With a flourish, again like the magician's next move, Ed unwrapped the bottle and placed it very carefully next to the money. "This is how I got the money. One hundred and fifty-five dollars," he said proudly.

Beth looked puzzled. Cal looked angry.

"You've got some explaining to do, Ed. Let's have the answers to all of this. I don't like guessing games."

"Calvin! Just let the boy tell his story."

It took almost two hours but by then all, even Ed's father, were smiling incredulously.

"So this old thing's worth a lot of money?"

"Yes Dad. The perfect ones will bring around eighty-five bucks. I sold two as I said, but for some reason I kept this one. It's got a little crack below the neck here, so maybe sixty or so. I figure I can sell it any time. I really wanted to show one of them to you and Tom. Maybe when Junior and Jenny get home from over there in Lebanon I could show them too."

Beth's eyes were sparkling, but not from tears. Cal had a big grin too. "We've got some good news too, just like you have, Eddy," she said.

"What's the news?"

"Your brother is coming back to the U.S.A.!" she cried.

"But . . . but . . . I thought he was going to stay for a year or more. They're not sick are they?"

"Oh no, Eddie, you see . . ."

Cal broke in. "There's some kind of political trouble over there. All U.S. citizens have been ordered out. Junior thinks they'll be back in the

States by next week at the latest. Also, he says his company is going to pay all the divers off in full, even though the work hasn't been finished."

"Want to hear some even better news?" Beth bubbled. "All three of them are going to come *here* for about a week as soon as they get things settled in Louisiana! Oh, it's going to be so *wonderful!*"

"How soon do you think they'll be coming, Mom? I've got all the final copies of old Eli's diaries finished. Do you think I should mail them or just wait till he gets here?"

"Mail them Ed. Junior sure seems to enjoy that crazy stuff. You pack them up and I'll take them to the post office today. I've got some business in town anyway. While I'm gone, you get some hay down. I don't suppose there's any oil left for the tractor. That car of yours drink it all up?" Both Ed and Beth were glad Cal was finally sounding more like his former self this morning!

"Nope. I bought twelve cans before I started home. I'll take care of the tractor. Grease it too if you want. And here's the ten you loaned me."

"That's good Ed. Now go ahead and wrap up those diary pages. I want to get going pretty quick." He left for the shop.

"Mom, I want to go over and see Tom today. Do you think Dad will be mad if I go?"

"He won't be mad if he doesn't *know about it!* Get the hay down and take care of the tractor right now. You can run over to the

Dillons' after your dad leaves. Better get going!"

"I'll need to unload the car first. Some of Tom's stuff is still in there. His sleeping bag got kind of wet, so I'll need to dry it out before I return it."

"I'll take care of his sleeping bag for you. Why did Tom come home so soon?" his mother asked, clearing the table.

"He got homesick, I guess. To tell you the truth, I did too sometimes, especially after he left. But you know I wanted to try to find the treasure, so I stayed."

"I was homesick once," Beth mused, staring out of the kitchen window. "It was right after your father and I were married. Seems like it only lasted for a week or so, but it was the worst feeling I've ever had. Never bothered me since though. Now you go on!"

X   X   X

"That old bottle?" Tom asked in amazement. "Are you kidding me? That thing's worth sixty or seventy bucks?"

They had been sitting in Ed's car for two hours, the sun nearly down. "I wish I'd have stayed," Tom said as they drove toward his home. "That island sounds pretty neat. Do you suppose we could go back up there later this summer?"

"No way, Tom! My dad's been pretty decent lately, but with the beans and corn to come off later on, I better not even *mention*

Michigan again! But I'll tell you what. If I ever do get back to Beaver Island you can come along. If you want to."

"Listen Ed . . .I . . . uh . . . well, I'm really sorry . . ."

"About coming home early?"

"Yeah, that and about slugging you there in the park. . . ."

"Tom, you sure pack a wallop! Did you ever consider a boxing career?"

"But the main thing is," Tom stumbled along. "I wish I hadn't told your folks about you staying in Michigan after the picking was over. I couldn't help it! Your dad was really mad at my dad. They made me tell! Couldn't help it, Ed."

"Hey, forget it, buddy. As a matter of fact it actually worked out pretty well. I had a little what you might call 'confrontation' with my old man. Told him if he ever hit me again I was going to hit back. Maybe I'm wrong, but I think he kind of *approved!* Maybe it made me seem a little more like Junior, who knows? Anyway it's all over and I'm rich man, *rich!*" He laughed.

CHAPTER SIXTEEN

Another Treasure

"Let's get out of here," Junior whispered. "The baby needs to be changed. It's my turn to do it, but if I hide long enough Jenny will take care of it. Did you ever smell anything that bad?"

They hid out in the barn, sitting on the wagon tongue.

"How was the work over there in Lebanon?"

"To tell the truth," Junior sighed, "we never really got started right. Some sort of government SNAFU I guess. But boy did we have it made over there! Two servants, a fancy apartment, the whole shebang. Jenny got tired of it though. She missed her parents. I didn't tell the folks that in my letters. I missed mine too," he laughed, pushing Ed off the wagon tongue.

"There was an article in Dad's True Magazine last month about the frogmen. Did you happen to see it?" Ed asked, chewing on a piece of straw.

"No Ed, I didn't. I don't try to think about that stuff back there. Do you want to know anything about it?"

"Well not if you don't want to."

"Don't tell Mom any of this, you hear? I'll tell you about our biggest campaign, because you ought to know something about the military. Looks like things are getting messy over there in Korea, so you may have to be in it in a few years or so. You know where Korea is?" Ed didn't.

"What are you two up to out here? Not doing any *work* I'm sure!" Their dad stood in the doorway, eyeing them.

"Come on in, Pop. Pull up a hay bale and sit down," Junior laughed. "I told Eddie I'd tell him about the biggest campaign our unit ever took part in. You might as well hear it too. Mom's off limits to any of this, of course."

"If it bothers you to talk about all of that, you don't have to you know." Cal stayed standing but leaned against a barn beam.

"This may be all I ever say about it, but I want somebody to know the truth. The papers, the radio, Hollywood, all of them get a lot of it wrong, but I was *there!*"

Junior sat very still, elbows on his knees, his head sort of hanging down. He cleared his throat twice and began.

"After all our training and being shuttled all around the U.S., we headed out on the Atlantic. It was January, nineteen forty-four, and there's never been anything colder than that trip. Well come to think of it you must have got pretty cold yourself up there on Lake Michigan. Right, Ed? See, I told you to get snorkeling equipment. Works really well doesn't it?"

"Uh . . .well . . . gee Dad . . .I should have told you . . ."

"Don't bother. I knew what you had up your sleeve when we were up in Toledo buying that stuff. I looked in the boxes the day after you and Tom left. I figured you'd take everything."

"Well Dad I guess I . . ."

"You know what your crazy younger brother did, Junior? Dug a map out of the muzzle of that old muzzle-loader in the summer kitchen, went cherry picking for three weeks, then sneaked out to Beaver Island and found a shipwreck. Got the ideas from the old diaries he's been sending you. I swear I never thought he had it in him!" Cal was actually grinning!

"I know all about it, Pop. The kid's been sending me secret letters in the packages of translations. He pulled it off slick as a whistle too!" He punched Ed on the shoulder, but his smile faded as he began to speak again.

"Took us thirteen days to make the crossing. Ice froze on every part of the ship. A German U-boat was sighted tailing our convoy, but they never fired a torpedo. Probably waiting for something bigger, like a destroyer or a cruiser. So we were lucky that way. About everybody on board was sick. I got along o.k. with that as long as I could stand up. The stupid ensign thought everybody would feel better lying in their hammocks. So he gave us the order. I disobeyed whenever I could get away with it. It was too cold and rough to go on deck, and the smell of navy chow being cooked with steam . . Well enough of that. A lot of GI's really liked being in England, but our small unit was top secret, so they kept us bottled up most of the time. We practiced blowing up fake obstacles until we were really good at it. When the big day came, D-Day you know, we got there o.k., even though a lot of the landing craft got blown up before they even reached the shore. Our crazy boat driver, the 'bosun', ran us right up close. We got into our gear, packed all the explosives we could handle, and did our job. There were fourteen guys in my crew. Six of us got back, two badly wounded. I write to a couple of the guys sometimes. We did the best we could, trying to clear the way for the landing craft. An awful lot of men died that day . . . it was awful . . .I can't tell you . . ."

Junior stopped talking. For a moment nobody said anything. Then he looked up, tried to smile, and said, "So that was how I won World War Two!" They all relaxed a little.

"I'm glad you told us, Junior. I hope Ed never has to do anything like that but if he does he'll be able to go to you for help."

"Did anybody change the baby?" Junior asked.

"Your wife did," Cal answered, "but she said it wasn't her turn. I wonder whose turn it was."

"Gosh! I have no idea. Let's go in for lunch."

        X   X   X

Supper over, the entire family gathered in the living room. Beth was trying to look happy, but she hated to think of Junior and his wife and baby leaving in the morning. "Well everybody, I have an important announcement to make, so listen up!" Junior said.

"Oh Junior, you're going to be moving back to Ohio! I'm *so glad!*"

"No. Sorry Mom. That's not it."

"Another baby's on the way! That's wonderful!"

"Wrong again. Well I *think* it's wrong." They all laughed as Jenny blushed prettily.

"What is it, son?"

"Dad, Mom, Eddie, just listen to this. You're not going to believe it."

"Junior for Pete's sake, tell us what's going on." Ed blurted.

"You know yesterday when I took my, I mean Ed's, car into town? Well I made a long distance call to a company in Baton Rouge." He stopped and made eye contact with each one in turn.

"Junior, you're driving them crazy. Just tell them what's up, will you?" Jenny chided him.

"Oh all right. The company I called is Markham-Westerlake, a big book publishing house. One of the part-time secretaries at our Deep Water Enterprises office is a college student who wants to be a writer. As a sort of joke I showed her one of Ed's 'translations' of old Eli's diaries. She got very excited and said . . ."

"She's very pretty too!" Jenny sniffed.

"Not nearly as pretty as you though." Junior said gallantly.

"Go on with the story," Calving said, grinning.

"I mean she got excited about the diaries! Nothing else! The girl told me I ought to send a couple of those pages to Markham-Westerlake. In one of her journalism classes they'd had to research various publishers to get an idea what each one of them wanted from authors. That particular one specialized in true historical material, especially first person accounts!"

"So he sent some, they wanted to see more, and they want to publish them *in a book!*" Jenny said.

"Hey, this is *my story*," Junior growled.

"It's getting late and we have to be up early tomorrow. At the rate you're telling this it will be midnight till we get to bed."

"O.k., O.k. So Mom, if you're in agreement they'll be sending you a contract, permission forms, and so forth. They mentioned a possible advance of five hundred dollars, plus a royalty of eight percent on the purchase price of every book sold. All of this has to be negotiated of course. You should have a lawyer look over the stuff before you sign anything."

No one said a word. They were completely stunned!

"Before you all faint on me, there's even better news."

"Junior, I can hardly believe all this. Why didn't you tell us sooner?"

"Because, Mom, when I was growing up, I remember you always telling us, 'I never heard a hen cackle until she had done her job'! I only got the final confirmation on that phone call, two days ago."

"Now get *this,* Eddie, little brother. Both of Eli's diaries together are not enough for a book. The publisher wants to tell *your* story right along with old Eli's. Can you imagine that?"

"My story? What do you mean? I don't get it."

"You will, kiddo, you will. They'll be interviewing you some time this fall, either by phone or in person. Then, guess what? They'll send the whole family up to Beaver Island to photograph you in the tent, snorkeling over the wreck, selling the bottles, everything you did. Of course I humbly offered my services for all underwater photography. So they'll fly me, Jenny, and the baby up there too."

"What bout the farm work?" Cal asked, trying to make sense of all of this.

"Don't worry, Dad. They'll pay for all the help you need. And, as far as I know they won't be doing the part up there in Michigan until later. Crops should all be in by then, but you wouldn't really have to go along if you didn't want to."

"I'm going!" their dad exclaimed. He clapped Ed on the knee. "This kid is a real go-getter! I guess we all owe him a big thank you."

"Cal, we really need to get to bed!" Jenny complained.

The baby was the only one who slept much.

CHAPTER 17

Back to Beaver Island

The summer was unusually busy. The crops were not as good as Cal hoped, as it was too dry most of the summer, then at harvest time it rained and rained!

"Don't worry, dear. According to the lawyer all the papers were in good order when I signed them in July. The five hundred dollar advance is right in the bank, and hopefully, when the book comes out there'll be even more money coming in. We're going to be fine!"

"You mean *if* that book gets published. When are they supposed to be here for the photographs and stuff?" Cal growled.

"This coming Tuesday. The letter said they would need a full day interviewing Eddie, the pictures to be taken at the same time. Oh I do wish I could have put some curtains up in that old summer kitchen. I've got those pink and yellow ones that used to hang here in the parlor. All I'd need to do is hem them up a little. And those cupboards out there! *Mercy!* They're full of old fruit jars. I wanted to clean the shelves, put some pretty shelf paper on them, then arrange my stoneware crock collection right up there. It would have looked so nice."

"Beth! Listen to yourself. You know Junior said none of us were to touch one thing out there. They want pictures that are authentic, not something that looks like the governor's dining room. You sure the school is o.k. with Eddie missing a full week of classes? Seems pretty odd to me that they're going to allow that."

"Calvin, he will have to make up some of the work, but they're thrilled about the book. The principal said it could be a real learning experience for the boy."

"What was that about putting up the tent here on the farm?"

"We're to have it up and arranged the way Tom and Ed used it in Michigan. They said any place where there are some bushes and trees would be good enough. That will save them time up on the island. I suppose the best place would be back in our woods somewhere don't you?"

"Is Tom Dillon going to Michigan with us?" Cal complained.

"No dear. I told you. His grades are not good enough. His parents won't let him go. But the publisher has agreed to take some pictures of him and Eddie around the tent. That's another reason for putting the tent up here in our woods."

"Sounds like a whole lot of foolishness to me," Cal said, but he was having trouble hiding his own excitement about the venture. He had not had a real vacation in several years. "Junior's to meet us up there, right?"

"Yes. That way he can have everything ready ahead of time."

"Ready for what? I'm getting confused by all this."

"He needs to rent a boat, get all his diving equipment checked out, and take a lot of underwater pictures. It's too bad Jenny and the baby won't be going, but they thought it was too much trouble, especially since Jenny's expecting again. She'll be dividing the week between me and her parents. I'm really looking forward to that!" Beth said, her smile lighting her face.

X   X   X

Ed had to laugh a little as he read Earl's letter. The third one he'd received, it was much like the first two, and very much like Earl himself!

Hi Ed. How are you? I'm o.k. Mom's got a boyfriend and maybe they'll get married petty soon. Mom says no but I think yes [?] He's o.k. I guess. Don't drink or says he don't anyway. Guess what? I got my learner's permit last week. Ralph, that's Mom's guy, takes me to the city park and lets me practice driving. He's a pretty good teacher and we go in his car! It's Nash Rambler. I'm gonna get me one just like it if I can get the money. [Or maybe a 35 Ford like yours.] I sure had a good time on Beaver this summer and guess what my asthma's been a lot better! The doctor says I should probably go up there every summer. Wouldn't that be too bad!! Ha ha Maybe you could come up there too sometimes. I know you got chores and farm work so maybe not but think about it o.k.? I can't play basketball like you do but Coach picked me to do the stats for the team. Get into all the games free and ride the team bus to the away ones. Pretty neat huh? Best news for me I got on the debating team. One of my teachers said I'd be perfect for it since I'm smart [fooled her haha] and never stop talking. Guess that's me alright at least the last part. We won 2 of our first 3 matches and hope to get into the city-wide tournament. We'll see.

How is the book coming? Did they take all those pictures of you, the old gun, the diaries, and everything? When do you go to Beaver Island? Say hello to my grandparents when you get up there. Wish I could go. Boy you really kept things quiet about getting those old bottles from the wreck. I guess you had to because like they said during the war, "loose lips sink ships". Of course the Caroline was already sunk! Haha. Our school usually takes two weeks off for Christmas vacation. What about yours? Would it be o.k. if I came down to your place then? Ralph said maybe I could even drive part of the way. Mom and him would come too, but it would only be for a day. We'd eat in a restaurant or something so no problem for your folks. Ralph says I'm a good driver, but then what would he say to the kid of a woman he might marry some time? Ha ha. Ralph is o.k. [for now at least]. Would you write back? I've kept your other letter. Tell me all about the book and how it's coming along. Save me three copies, autographed of course! So long for now. Your Beaver Island pal, Earl.

Hi Earl, got your letter so thanks for it. Things are really hopping around here. We're about ready to go. Dad's o.k. with my buddy, Tom, and his dad doing the farm work while we're gone. Hope old Curly don't kick the bucket for Tom! The pictures went real well although they probably broke a couple cameras on me!

Mom says you and your mom and Ralph are to come right down here any time during the holidays. You better not even *think* about eating in some restaurant [she says] because you'll all have a noon meal right here. She says "noon meal" because she says when some people say "dinner" they mean what we call "supper"! I don't care what it's called as long as there's plenty of food. Ha ha.

My friend Tom is pretty excited about the book too. They took a picture of him pretending to shave by our tent, which was set up back in our woods, don't ask me why. And also because they photographed his copy of the map I dug out of Eli's muzzle loader. Mom's all bent out of shape about the pictures they took in the old summer kitchen. She wanted to put up curtains and stuff! They said they wanted it to look just the way it did when I was out there messing with that old gun. When you come [if that works out I mean] I'll show you that place and we can walk the creek where I have my trap line during the season. Won't be able to show you the book though. They're planning to have it out some time in March. Glad your doctor said Beaver Island would be good for your summers. Maybe I could get up there too, but don't count on it. *The farm* you know! Rats!

I made the basketball team again, but still not getting to play much. Got a sore behind from all the bench sitting! Ha ha. Hey, Earl, write some more. I like to get your letters. Don't drive that Nash Rambler over 95 m.p.h., O.k.? Later --- Ed.

"Is everything all set for us to be gone for five days?" Ed asked his mother as he cranked the cream separator.

"I believe it is, Eddie. Your father is just full of surprises these days. You probably know that he's asked Tom and his father to do chores and take care of things while you're gone. Of course I'll be here anyway, but your dad says to let them do the chickens and everything while they're here every day. Isn't it wonderful that all he has to do is pay them, then send the amount to the publisher. They'll reimburse us for every penny!"

"Not only that, Mom, but they're paying all of Dad's and my expenses too. They must really think this book is going to be a good seller. Hope it turns out that way. What did you think of the pictures they took?"

"They were very good of you, and that one of Tom by the tent pretending to shave was a classic, even if our woods probably look nothing like Beaver Island. But I shudder every time I think of possibly hundreds of people looking at the pictures taken in that old summer kitchen! If they'd only have let me spruce it up a little."

"Now Mom, you know they wanted those shots to 'look authentic' as they put it. They just raved at the idea of that little cabin being the very one that Eli and his Family lived in for a while. I can see how they looked at it, don't you?" Ed said.

"Oh I guess so . . . but I can't see how a few curtains and a good scrubbing would have hurt anything. Jenny said . . ."

Cal came into the kitchen, glanced at them, and sort of lingered by the sink where Ed was scalding the many parts of the separator. "Uh, . . .Beth . . .where did you put them pictures those guys took?"

"They're on the end table by the couch. I told you that."

"I don't know why they had to take my picture in the barn pretending to milk. Why it was in the middle of the day! I had a new white shirt and everything too. They could have taken my picture right in our living room. I told them that, but they never even acted like they heard me. Did you pack that shirt and tie for me? Maybe they'll take a decent picture of me on that island."

Beth and Ed grinned at each other as Cal headed for the living room. He was *hooked!*

X   X   X

The weather cooperated better than they could have hoped. Cal didn't get seasick at all, and Ed had only a little funny felling in his stomach. Junior met them at the dock and took them to the small hotel where he was staying. After they had eaten lunch right in the hotel, Junior drove them down to South Shores in his rented pickup.

A yellow inflatable ring was bobbing up and down right over the wreck site. Junior wasted no time getting into his wet suit and SCUBA equipment. "Come on," he yelled, launching the boat he'd rented.

"Better take off your shoes and socks. You'll need to wade for a little ways till she floats free."

"What's all this?" Ed asked, eyeing the junk on the deck.

"Stuff I've been bringing up. I've made a bunch of dives since I got here. All the pictures they wanted are done, so I'm treasure hunting! Eddie, I can't imagine how you were able to dive out here without a wet suit! The water must have been *freezing!* It's cold enough now!"

"Find anything valuable down there?" Cal asked bluntly. "This stuff just looks like trash to me."

"I'm afraid that's all it is so far," Junior replied ruefully. "As long as this calm weather holds though, I'll be going down some more. I've been trying to lift a couple heavy beams that may open up something good. They're loose, but too heavy to move much."

Cal looked thoughtful. "What you need is a block and tackle. Throw a noose around one of the beams, then hook one end to your boat. Every time the boat drops a little from the waves, cinch it up. I bet that will get the timber up enough that you could see what's under it."

"By golly Dad, that's great idea! With all our frogman training we never learned anything like that. Let's go to the village and see if we can rent an outfit like that for a couple days."

After supper at the hotel two days later, Junior looked around at the other diners. "Let's go out to the truck. I need to talk to Ed, but not in here. Too many eyes and ears!"

"I got up early this morning and sneaked out before you two were even *thinking* about leaving your warm beds. I wanted to get out to the wreck while it was still real calm. The block and tackle worked fine this time. I didn't even need any wave action. Just kept hauling away and snubbing the rope each time the log rose a few inches. All at once that log shifted and slid off to the side. I kept my rope tied, suited up, and went down. Eddie, I felt like you must have felt when you saw those bottles."

"What do you mean, Junior?" Ed asked in almost a whisper.

"Well little brother, it was *bottles!* Most of them were pretty well smashed up, but I got *six whole ones!*"

"Six!" Ed yelled.

"Quiet kid! They were all in a row, side by side. Must have been in a case once, but the wood was long gone."

"Eli's diaries told about *lots* of cases!" Ed hissed.

"Maybe so, but sand has drifted in over the years and filled everything in. It would take big money to get to whatever is left down there. I'm afraid these six are the last we're going to get. Some of them may be chipped a little."

"Junior, do you know what Eddie here got paid for just a couple of those old things?" Cal asked incredulously.

"That I do, Dad. That I do! Seventy or eighty bucks each. We're talking at least four hundred and fifty dollars here! Maybe more if we can find a buyer."

"Find a *buyer?*" Ed yelled. "The lady I sold mine to said she'd buy any more I can come up with. Man, we have hit the jackpot, thanks to old Eli and his diaries. I hope he's looking down at us right now. His map and journals did the job!

They caught the ferry the next morning, and headed for home.

The end.